THE PIRATES OF PENN COVE

WEIRDBEY ISLAND
BOOK I

ELDRITCH BLACK

The Pirates of Penn Cove

CONTENTS

NOTE TO READER

Beware of this tale. Such *stories* should never be told. As those in the know would tell you, the terrible events revealed in these pages are quite real. They happened.

We pleaded with the author to burn the manuscript, but he refused. We warned him the story is unsafe, but he ignored our pleas. Admittedly he disguised some names and altered a few locations, but those efforts were nowhere near enough to make this book safe and ultimately we found these adjustments as useful as a hat made of soup.

Such secrets as these should be kept. And now you're about to learn them, so take good care of yourself. Sleep with one eye open. Look over your shoulder. Check the shadows, they're not as they seem.

Read on at your peril.

Our deepest sympathies,
    The Society of the Owl and Wolf

1

WEIRDBEY ISLAND

It was too much. I was ready to explode. I'd been stuck in the backseat of the car for six hours straight trying to ignore my brother's almost constant harassment, and something was about to give.

Even though Jamie was twelve, the same age as me, he always had to point out that he was actually ten months older. A technicality, but he decided it meant he got to tell me what to do. And where I was as skinny as a beanpole, he was a wall of muscle, which didn't help.

Jamie ran and played football in his spare time; I read.

We had the same sea-green eyes and crazy wavy brown hair, but his was cut as short as a soldier's, while mine sprouted like weeds. I couldn't be bothered with stuff like that.

Between us sat Wilson, our dog, a super enthusiastic foxhound with seriously bad breath. He was snoring and the long string of drool hanging from his lower lip was about to fall on the floor.

I shifted in my seat as Mom pulled up to the toll booth and paid the man in the window, then we drove down into the ferry lot. We parked at the end of a long row of cars and all I could see around us were lines and lines of even more cars, their roofs shining in the sunlight.

There was noise everywhere; gulls, buzzing wasps, people laughing, shouting, yelling, and heavy booming music. The air smelled of seaweed, hot tarmac, and fries.

Mom and Dad leaned over and kissed each other. I glanced past them and the grey-white splodges of dead bugs streaked across the windshield, to the distant island.

Whidbey Island. Our new home.

It looked like a big strip of green forest floating in the water. I could just about make out a few tiny houses along a beach and above them trees, trees and more trees sprouting from the hillsides. In the distance, beyond the island, were huge mountains, jagged and dark against the deep blue sky.

"Hey, can I get an ice cream?" Jamie asked as he pulled his head back in through the window.

"Sure." Dad handed us a wad of worn dollar bills. He wasn't usually that generous, but I got the feeling he and mom wanted *alone time*. Which was gross.

"Thanks." I flashed a goofy smile as I took the money. We'd been driving for two days, leaving our home behind as well as the only friends I had in the whole wide world. To make matters worse, I'd lost the charger for my phone and I'd never actually written down Sam or Caden's numbers, which meant I was totally alone.

I got out of the car. The sky was bright, the sun golden and fierce. A wall of heat rose up from the pavement as I walked along the line of cars toward the snack bar by the ferry dock and got in line. I was three people behind Jamie, but that suited me fine.

When it was my turn, I ordered a double-chocolate from a girl with an angry voice and more freckles than I'd ever seen. Then I walked over and stood by the dock, eating my ice-cream and as I looked out over the water, or the Sound, as Mom said it was called, I froze.

A row of puffy dark clouds hovered over the island. They definitely hadn't been there when I'd looked before and a thick smudge of grey sea mist was rolling across the water.

None of it looked like it could be real. It seemed impossible that the weather could change that quickly, but it had.

"Hey!" I jumped as something squawked in my ear and a ragged black shape shot past my face. It was a crow; a *huge* crow with glinting eyes and a long curved beak. It wheeled around and flew straight at me. I dropped my ice-cream onto the chippy white wooden rungs of the pier as I ducked. Then another crow swept down, grabbed the cone and took off. The first bird followed, cawing. It was like they'd just tag teamed me. "Hey!" I shouted again.

"Ha! You got robbed!" Jamie appeared behind me laughing, a stupid fat grin growing on his face. "By a bird! Loser!"

"Shut up, Jamie!" I turned back to the water and watched the old white ferry loaded with people and cars approach the dock. Behind it, the clouds that hung over the island seemed to have grown even heavier.

"We're on our way to Weirdbey Island," Jamie said, shaking his head. "We'll probably die there."

"It's Whidbey," I said, correcting him even though there was no point. His shadow fell over me as he clamped a meaty hand on my shoulder.

"Yeah, that's what it says on the signs. But its real name is Weirdbey Island, Dyllyboo." He'd been calling me Dyllyboo for as long as I could remember and the novelty hadn't worn off. For him at least. "I read about it online."

"Good for you."

"Yeah, it was all pretty boring until I finally found the

honest sites. The ones talking about the stuff the tourism people don't want you to know about."

"You're lying." I yawned with pretend boredom but he had my attention, and we both knew it.

"Am I?" He released his hand from my shoulder. "Yeah, you're probably right. So there's probably no point in telling you what I found out, is there?"

I shook my head but curiosity got the better of me, just like it always did. "So what did it say? On those websites?" I tried but failed to sound only mildly interested.

"Well, as far as wildlife is concerned, you only have to worry about mountain lions, bears and rattlesnakes."

"That's not true." Was it?

"And then, there's the Bigfoots. You can read about them for yourself, just look it up. No doubt you'll run into one soon enough."

"You're lying." But as I glanced back to the patch of sea mist and the heavy grey clouds, I shivered, despite the heat. It wasn't exactly difficult for me to get scared, even though I tried my hardest not to.

"Did you see that fog? It doesn't look good, Dyllyboo," Jamie continued. "Maybe the ferry will crash into rocks, or an iceberg or something. Then you'll drown. I'll probably make it to shore. If I do, you can count on me to help carry your coffin at the funeral."

"Shut up." It wasn't funny. I hated the water, and he knew it. I could swim, I loved to swim, in swimming pools. But the ocean freaked me out. It was dark and deep and full of horrible things, like sharks and worse. And now we were about to live on an island surrounded by it. Great.

"Sorry, Dylan. I forgot you don't like the sea. Here." He offered me his ice-cream. "We're in this together, bro."

Like a fool, I reached for it. He snatched it away and gave

his stupid super-villain laugh. I turned away from the water and our almost certain doom, and trudged back to the car, glad for the AC at least.

"Where's your ice-cream?" Mom asked. Her lipstick was smudged and her eyes gleamed like they always did when she and Dad got all smoochy.

"It flew away," Jamie said.

The cars around us started up. I gazed ahead as we slowly drove down toward the ferry, ignoring Jamie as he slurped the last of his ice-cream and crunched through the cone. I hated him.

We parked and once all the cars had stopped, I climbed out to get away from Jamie, who was burping and blowing his breath at me.

Mom locked the car, and we strode up the stairs. The ferry began to rumble and shake. As soon as we reached the top deck, I wandered off to get away from them. They sat at a table and looked out the window. I found a spot on the other side of the deck next to some strangers with little kids and a shrieking baby.

The ferry had pulled away and I was glad, I wanted to get our doomed voyage over with as soon as possible. Slowly, the island drew toward us along with the clouds and rolling sea mist. Rain spattered the window, and the air turned cool.

I looked back. Behind us was a sunny summer's day and somehow, it seemed like it was a world away.

The baby began howling louder than ever, so I moved to the back of the ferry and went out onto the deck where people stood posing for photographs, the wind whipping up their hair.

I leaned on the rail and glanced over the side as the propeller churned the deep blue water into a white froth. I felt sick, like my insides were churning too, but I forced myself to stay there. I had to get over my fears. I had to show Jamie I wasn't scared. Maybe then he'd stop hassling me.

"What?" I mumbled as something broke the surface of the water. A great big rubbery tentacle. It curled into the air as if searching for prey, and then it slipped back down and vanished into the dark water.

A moment later I saw a massive shape below the water. It was easily the size of a house and had two round milky-blue eyes and a ton of pulsing tentacles. It was an octopus. A *giant* octopus.

My heart hammered as I glanced around to check if anyone else had seen it, to make sure I wasn't losing my mind. The beast moved off and disappeared into the murk.

I strode back inside, my heart pounding and my arms and legs shaking like jelly. Everyone looked, calm. People read on their phones, the baby still wailed. It seemed no one besides me had seen the monster.

"Dylan!" Dad strode over, adjusting his glasses. He smiled through his beard like there wasn't a problem in the world. I guess there wasn't, for him at least. "You okay?" His thick eyebrows knitted together.

No. I wasn't okay, but I forced a smile. "Sure."

There was no point telling him what I'd seen, he wouldn't believe it. No one would. We trudged back down to our car as the engines slowed and a tinny voice came through the speakers announcing we'd almost reached the island.

I climbed into the backseat, still thinking about the creature.

Maybe Jamie hadn't been lying about monsters? That thing was down there somewhere, underneath the dark water, its tentacles large enough to capsize the ferry.

I glanced out the window as the island drew closer. A rolling curtain of sea mist swept toward us. Surely this couldn't be normal... Suddenly, Wilson began to whine and his ears flattened over his head.

The mist broke and for a moment I saw a great ship at its center. It looked old, like the boats people sailed in hundreds of years ago. Its wooden hull was festooned with straggly seaweed and encrusted with thousands of bone white barnacles. Ghostly lights glowed at the bow, and then, as the mist parted once more, I saw the silhouette of a huge man. He wore a crumpled triangular hat, his beard shimmered like it was full of fireflies, and it felt like he was staring right back at me.

The ship was sailing in fast. Way too fast. It was headed right at the ferry!

❧ 2 ❧

THE THING IN THE TREES

"I t's going to hit us!" I shouted and grabbed the car door, bracing myself for the crash. Time slowed and silence fell. It was the calm before the storm.

I waited and waited, hoping Mom, Dad, and even Jamie were prepared for the impact, and that we'd make it through this impending disaster.

"That's it! He's officially lost his mind," Jamie announced, then he sighed theatrically. "It was only a matter of time."

I opened my eyes, not even realizing I'd closed them.

The ship was gone. So was the mist. Like they'd never been there.

Mom and Dad stared at me. They looked worried. Jamie was grinning but even he seemed surprised by my outburst.

The ferry continued gliding smoothly toward the dock. I climbed out of the car, raced to the railing and peered out over the side.

The cool air caused my arms to break out into goosebumps. "There! It's right over there!" I called, but no one was listening. The strange mist was drifting off into the distance, but I could still make out the dark outline of the ship within it.

How had it gotten past the ferry? It had looked like it was going to crash right through us... Perhaps it had managed to swerve around us at the last moment, while my eyes were shut. But as for the ship itself, why had it looked so old? Was it a relic from a museum? Was the man with the strange hat a historical actor or something?

"Dylan!" Mom called. I walked back, my face burning hot, my head hanging down like a dog waiting to be scolded for snatching food off the table. "Are you okay?" She looked worried.

"Yeah, I... I thought I saw..." I shook my head and forced a smile. It was pretty obvious no one else had seen the ship.

"Come on. I think we've all been cooped up in the car for a bit too long," Mom said as she led me back. "And they say moving is one of the most stressful times for people. But we're almost there and we'll be unpacking and settling in before you know it."

I climbed back in and buckled up, ignoring Jamie as he stared and twirled his finger at the side of his head.

The ferry docked with a bump, the car juddered and after what felt like forever, our lane began to drive off. Soon we were on the dock driving past another jam-packed lot of waiting cars toward a massive wooden sign that read:

'Welcome to Whidbey Island.'

I didn't feel welcome. I felt totally lost.

"Did you see that?" Jamie asked as the engine shifted and groaned up the steep hill.

I peered out his window. The trees were huge, the biggest I'd ever seen. I wondered what would happen in a hurricane. Trees like that could easily crush the car in two, and us with it. "See what?" I asked as the scent of pine wafted in.

"Oh, I don't know... I think it might have been a mountain lion. It was eyeing the car and licking its lips," Jamie said.

"Don't listen to him," Dad said. "Jamie, stop trying to scare your brother, he should be happy, not frightened. We're here." His grin swelled up around his beard. "Our new home. It's exciting!"

Exciting? The word I'd have picked was *horrible*. It seemed to me like we were trapped on a lost chunk of rock in the middle of the sea.

We stopped at the traffic lights and turned onto a long straight road. The sun dappled through the trees and I realized the place was very pretty with its woodlands, orchards and pastures, and shades of green everywhere I looked. I imagined riding my bike, that might be fun. Of course, it would have been more fun with Sam and Caden, but they were back home and I was stuck in this island wilderness with my idiot brother, possibly forever.

Finally, we reached Langley, a village with a long street of neat, old fashioned wooden shops, an old brick school and a little theater. After the quick buzz through town we took a few turns and made our way up a long dirt road that ran alongside meadows and pastures as it led us toward a forest filled with even more gigantic trees. The space below them turned almost black as the clouds doused the sun. For a moment it seemed like summer was over, even though it was almost the beginning of July.

Mom had shown us the house at least a million times on her phone, but it looked so different in real life. Bigger, more real. One of the first things I noticed was that the woods were way closer to the house than I'd thought. Way closer than they'd looked in the photos.

The neighbor's mailboxes were farther down the dusty road but I couldn't see any of their houses through the trees. I didn't like that at all; what if we needed help in the middle of the night? What if there was an emergency? A bear attack...

I grabbed my backpack and followed Jamie inside.

Our furniture and all the stuff we'd packed had already been delivered to the house. There were boxes everywhere I looked. Aunt Sabrina and Uncle Troy had come by to let the movers in. It looked like they'd tried to stack and organize the boxes and make the place seem more homey but it was like a labyrinth. All it needed was a Minotaur.

I followed Jamie upstairs.

"This is my room," he announced as if it had already been decided. Mom and Dad had taken the room at the front of the house so there was only one room left.

I was about to protest Jamie's claim and suggest we toss a coin for it, but then I realized the last room might actually be better. For one thing, it was at the far end of the house and tucked away from sight. It had that going for it at least. "Fine." I wandered down the hall and entered my new bedroom.

It was larger than my last one. One wall sloped down from the ceiling but I could still fit my TV along the shortened wall. There was already a desk in the corner and my old bed was there too, so I guessed someone had already decided this was my room already. It looked so strange and out of place. I glanced out the window to find spindly scratchy branches and a billion or more places along the edge of the woods where a wolf or maniac could hide.

I rolled my eyes. My imagination seemed to be in overdrive, probably from being trapped in the car with Jamie for so long.

"Dylan!" Dad's voice echoed up from downstairs. I tossed my backpack on the bed and put my phone on the empty desk. The screen was black, the battery dead, and I had serious doubts it would ever come back to life.

WE SPENT ALL AFTERNOON MOVING BOXES FROM ONE ROOM to another and unpacking. Slowly, things started to fall into place, like the house was a giant puzzle.

Aunt Sabrina and Uncle Troy came over and they brought pizzas. I liked both of them a lot, even though Aunt Sabrina was a bit strange. She had a mass of wiry hair like me and mum, and big red lips that sometimes pouted like a fish.

Uncle Troy was as quiet as my aunt was loud. She talked more than anyone I'd ever known, while most of the time he barely said a word. His eyes would shift as he followed the conversations and for some weird reason, he often made me think of a ferret in an overcoat. When he did get chatty, his favorite subject was the worms he kept in his wormery, which wasn't exactly the most interesting thing to have to hear about for the hundredth and fiftieth time.

After dinner, Sabrina and Troy left and I went upstairs to read a book.

I was almost at the end of the hallway, which was swimming in shadows, when the closet door swung open. Its hinges creaked like a tired old man. I froze and studied the door and the murk inside. "Jamie?" I called.

It was getting dark outside, and the inside of the closet was like a pitch black rectangle. "That's not funny," I added.

Where was he? I hadn't seen him for ages. Usually, he slunk away when Sabrina and Troy showed up. He found them boring, except around Christmas or right before his birthdays of course, then he couldn't get enough of them.

Something wheezed in the closet. Like heavy, ragged breathing. "Wilson!" I called. There was a scatter of paws from the kitchen and drumming thuds as Wilson ran up the stairs. He stood beside me, staring up, his tail wagging as if we were playing a game. "Get him!" I pointed to the door. His ears went flat as he glanced toward it. He was an even bigger wimp than I was.

"Thanks for the support." I crept down the hall but Wilson wouldn't budge, even his tail was still.

I'd almost reached the closet when the door sprang open and a monster jumped out.

My scream caught in my throat and my legs turned to water.

A moment later, I saw past the warty green skin to my brother's stupid eyes. He gave a shrill, idiotic laugh, tore off the mask and threw it at me. I ducked and it sailed over my head.

"You're such a coward, bro," Jamie said.

I shook my head. My fright turned to a hot flash of anger. "Moron!"

Jamie patted Wilson, who had jumped almost as high as I had. "Your problem is you've got no sense of humor," Jamie said, "and," he continued, "you *are* a coward. You're scared of everything! You need to toughen up and learn how to stand up for yourself."

"Like this?" I shoved him in the chest. It was a stupid move. He could flatten me in seconds if he wanted to and we both knew it.

Jamie shook his head. "I can't believe we're related. You must have been switched at birth." He patted my head, messing up my already messed up hair and strode to his room.

I stood in the middle of the hall, mad as ever. Part of me wanted to go after him and pummel him with my fists, but fighting wasn't my thing. I lost every single time.

My gaze drifted to the window at the end of the hallway. Night was falling. I probably should have been in bed at least an hour ago but the rules seemed to have been put on hold during the move.

Wilson groaned and his tail swished over the carpet as his ears rose high. He needed to go out.

"Great." I trudged downstairs and opened the front door. Cool air drifted in as he followed me out. Everything seemed fine. Then Wilson scampered across the yard and vanished into the woods.

"Hey!" I ran after him. "Come back!" I could hear him sniffing and snorting and crashing through the undergrowth. Bushes waved and rustled, and then everything fell still.

I gazed up into the trees, past the branches to the dim grey smudge of the sky. Maybe, I thought, this place wasn't so bad after all. It was kind of neat, having our own bit of forest, and-

Someone whistled in the woods. Then I heard a growl.

"Wilson!" I shouted as something bolted through the bushes, right toward me.

❧ 3 ❧
WORMS AND FOG

My scream stuck in my throat. The thing running at me was Wilson. His ears were flat and his tail was low between his legs. Something else was plowing through the brush behind him. It was getting closer and closer. A deer? It didn't sound like an animal to me; it was too clumsy.

It sounded like a person.

Who would be walking through the woods at this time of night? What was that whistling about? And why had everything gotten so quiet?

"Come on, boy," I called to Wilson as I tramped back across the dirt road to the house. Wilson shoved his way through the door before me, and I closed it quickly behind us.

I said goodnight to my parents, bounded up the stairs, drew my curtains and flopped onto the bed. It seemed like the entire world had gone crazy. The octopus, the ghost ship, and now some maniac lurking in the woods outside our house.

Jamie was right, I *was* a wimp. Pretty much everything scared me and even I was getting sick of it.

The hum of Mom and dad's conversation drifted up through the floor, but it didn't bother me. No, what bothered me was the wedge of dark sky I could see through the gap in the curtains and the thought of what might be lurking out there.

NOTHING HAPPENED THAT NIGHT. I DIDN'T WAKE TO FIND my whole family gone or a crazed maniac standing over my bed, but that was what I dreamt about.

I opened the curtains to find a warm sunny day. We spent most of the morning unpacking, but by the end of it, there was still a maze of crates and boxes everywhere I looked.

Then, after lunch, Mom announced she was heading to a place called Oak Harbor to go shopping. She asked if I wanted to go with her so I could look for a phone charger. I foolishly agreed and after a very long drive and three hours searching what felt like hundreds of stores, I still didn't have a hope or chance of getting reconnected to the rest of civilization.

Worse, on our way home, while we were zipping past a wide cove dotted with stilted rickety old buildings and jetties propped up over the glittering blue water, mom's phone rang.

A second later my aunt's voice blared through the speaker. Within moments they were chatting away as if they hadn't spent the entire previous night gabbing to each other. I tried to read my book, but it was impossible to concentrate.

"You're already in the car, so just come over," my aunt said, "I've made a huge avocado salad. You know how you like avocado!"

"I should get home, Ben and Jamie probably haven't eaten anything except chips, or toast. Or chips on toast."

"What difference will half an hour make? I want to show you those earrings I made."

No. Please no, I thought. I wanted to go home. I'd made a

deal with Jamie to take over his dish-washing duties for the week in exchange for an hour's gaming on his console.

"You don't mind if we pop over to see Aunty Sabrina, do you?" Mom asked me. "We won't be long."

What could I say? "Yeah, that's fine."

৩১৯

SABRINA AND TROY'S HOUSE WAS RIGHT ON THE BEACH. IT was big but old and kind of rundown. The front yard was filled with my uncle's wormery bins and the back of the house faced the sea. The tide was out, and the dark sand stretched off into the distance.

It looked like a good place to find skipping stones. I liked to collect them along with strangely colored pebbles and sea glass too when I could find it. "I might go for a walk," I said as they finished their salad and there was a short pause in the conversation.

"Off for an adventure?" Uncle Troy asked as he glanced up from the recliner where he sat watching a documentary about the life cycle of earthworms.

I nodded. Adventure? Probably not. A quiet walk away from the endless chatter? Definitely.

The day was still warm but a cool breeze swept off the water. It was hazy but I could see an island across the water. It was called Marrowstone Island according to my uncle. Behind it I could see the Olympic Mountains. They were so big and striking that they made the mountains back home look like silly little hills. As I thought this, I realized there was no *back home* anymore. That this was home now.

As soon as I reached a curve in the beach, I scanned the horizon and spotted two people digging in the sand. At first, I thought they were clamming. Uncle Troy had said that was common on this beach, but they didn't look like they were foraging for shellfish, they looked like they were digging with purpose.

I couldn't see them all that clearly because they were quite a way down the beach. But I could tell the woman was wearing a long coat, despite the heat, and the man had a huge belly and a thick bushy beard. And both of them had hats. His was like a sailor's cap and hers was some kind of beret.

They were bad news. I knew that right away. I headed toward the tree-line and watched them for a moment. They paused and looked around as if making sure they were alone.

What were they doing? Were they burying a body? Or digging one up? That was what it looked like but I couldn't see anything strange lying on the sand nearby. Then they suddenly stepped back, the shovels limp in their hands.

I shivered as the air turned cold and wisps of grey mist blew past me.

Behind me, a fog had swallowed up most of the beach. Everything looked grey and unearthly, and it felt more like winter than summer.

A bad smell wafted on the breeze. It made me think of damp and rot and old cellars in gloomy, dark houses. Somewhere, a distant bell clanged and something huge passed through the water, right by the beach.

It sounded like a ship.

I shuddered as I thought of the boat I'd seen from the ferry, and the creepy man in the pirate's hat standing on the deck. I looked back as footsteps trudged through the sand toward me. The diggers were running into the trees, clutching their shovels like they were rifles. Within moments they vanished into the mist.

A rickety din came from the waterline. Then, the creak of old ropes tightening and the groan of ancient, weathered boards. How could a boat pass by so close to shore? Surely the water was too shallow... I shook my head. Whatever was out there wasn't natural.

The bell rang again. It sounded even closer, like the boat was turning. The dark fog rolled toward me.

I ran, my sneakers sinking into the sand as I jumped over driftwood and raced away as fast as I could. I chanced a glance back. I couldn't see anything but the sea mist.

"No!" I cried, as the the sound of whatever was sailing through the water after me seemed to come from everywhere at once.

🦋 4 🦋
THE MIDNIGHT GARAGE SALE

I raced back to the house and flew through the door.

It was like passing into a different world; from chaos and danger to the dull, normal peace of a Sunday visit. Mom and Sabrina were still chatting, and Uncle Troy sat watching TV. It was like nothing had happened.

I glanced out the window. The ragged mist drifted like smoke as it passed the curve of the shoreline and vanished from view.

"See anything interesting?" my uncle asked as he paused the documentary and joined me by the window.

"There were these people digging," I said. "They were-"

"Clammers," he waved his hand, and by the tone of his voice, it was clear that he had no doubts at all. Or curiosity. It didn't involve worms so it wasn't of interest and I knew if I told him about the ship and mist, he'd probably think I was nuts. So I didn't say a word.

There was a brief pause in the chatter and Mom glanced over and promised we'd leave soon.

I still felt unsettled. The strangers digging, the eerie groaning sound of the ship sweeping along the beach, sailing in that weird fog. It had to be the same phenomenon from the day before. At least I hoped it was, because otherwise there was more than one of those creepy ships, and one was already troubling enough, especially on the heels of that enormous octopus...

It would have been better to ask about it, to have a grown-up tell me it was only my imagination, that it was normal or that octopus' were common here and perfectly harmless. But if I brought the subject up, it would just give my mom and Sabrina more fodder to yack about, and I really wanted to go home.

So I sat by the window and watched the clouds turn peach and red as the sun sank toward the mountains.

MOMENTS LATER I WOKE. MOM WAS SHAKING MY ARM. "What?" I sat up.

I'd fallen asleep and it was dark out. I glanced at the clock on the wall. It was almost midnight.

"Sorry, Dylan," Mom said. "I had no idea how late it was."

We left, and even though Aunt Sabrina still had plenty to say, we got to the car without Mom getting caught up in the conversation again.

The road was gloomy and clouds covered the moon. We drove in silence and it seemed Mom was all talked out. Then she spotted a handmade sign at the side of the road. Someone had painted 'Midnight Bazaar, 12 Sharp! Ends at 1.' in thick red flowing letters on its chipped wooden surface.

"What's a bazaar?"

"It's like a garage sale," Mom said.

A sinking feeling passed through me as her hands tightened

on the steering wheel and a grin lit her face. She glanced at me. "Just a quick look, I promise!"

I'd probably been to more garage sales than I'd eaten ham sandwiches, and I'd eaten *a lot* of ham sandwiches. Mom was hooked on rummage sales but I had to admit I was a little curious about this one myself. What kind of people had garage sales in the middle of the night? "Okay," I said.

"We won't be long," Mom said as we followed the next sign and took a right turn onto a road with a row of dark houses. At the end of the block was a blaze of lights and a tangle of parked cars. "You never know..." Mom said, "you might find a charger for your phone."

That was about as likely as a flurry of snow fluttering down from the starlit sky, but I agreed with her, it was easier that way. Besides, I really wanted to know who was holding this *midnight bazaar.* At least until we started to walk toward the house. It was kind of set back from the road and surrounded by dark, rustling trees. An owl hooted loud and slow, and suddenly I felt a strong sense of dread. Like things were about to go very wrong.

5

MONTGOMERY

Something scampered in the bushes. It could have been a rat, a chipmunk, or even a bear. A shiver broke across my arms and I pulled the long sleeves of my hoody over my hands like I always did when something was creeping me out.

We walked between the cars parked outside the house. The house's roof was high and sloping with a wonky brick chimney on one side. Its dark walls could have been any shade of black in the gloom. The porch light flickered, and the front door hung ajar as silhouettes moved past the curtains.

Mom didn't seem to notice how utterly sinister the place looked, in fact, she almost skipped to the front porch, her eyes wild with bargain fever. "Come on, Dylan!"

She pushed the creaky door open and stepped inside. I followed, dragging my feet as I went.

The house seemed even older and eerier inside. Faded green wallpaper curled along its seams and dark antique furniture filled the hall. There were weird things everywhere I looked. Wooden statuettes of monkeys and toads, carved monsters with big wings and fearsome claws, spooky old candles that looked like thin waxy fingers. There were creepy paintings; hooded figures, flaming eyes, people with bodies made of white frothy waves standing on beaches.

I didn't like any of it, but Mom seemed to think it was gothy and cool. She was strange that way.

Ten or more people stood around in the living room examining books, art prints and knick-knacks piled on tables and cabinets. Most of them were dressed strangely, like something from the olden days. They made me think of actors. It was as if they were pretending to shop, or putting on a play. I knew when people were faking, and these were fakers, every single one of them. Mom didn't notice, she just wandered over to a stack of books and began rifling through them.

Then I saw the man in the corner. He was tall, *really* tall, and he wore an old suit. The way he loomed and glanced around made him seem like the owner. He ran a hand over the few greasy strands of hair left on his balding head and then his watery blue eyes found mine and he smiled.

Something brushed my leg, and I looked down to find a cat the color of a dingy old mop. Its wide yellow-green eyes and the markings on its face made it look like an angry owl. It cried and gently bit my shin but as I stooped to stroke it, it trotted off through a doorway and turned back to glance at me.

So I followed it.

The cat padded down the short hall, then up the stairs. I didn't want to go up there, but the cat turned back to me and mewed, so up I went.

Doors lined the hallway on the second floor. The cat brushed one open and its tail slinked through the gap as it vanished inside. And then it meowed again. It was like it was calling me.

I followed it into a long wide room with a bed and a rickety old dresser. As I saw our car through the dusty window, I hoped we'd be leaving soon. The place was seriously giving me the creeps.

The cat yowled. I almost jumped out of my own skin. Then I saw what it wanted. Two silver bowls were sitting on the floor. One was filled with water and the other was empty. Beside it was a box of cat food, so I filled the bowl and stroked the cat, giving it a gentle pat. It purred as it ate.

I was about to head back downstairs when a heavy creak came from the hall.

Someone was outside the room, whispering. I peered through the crack and saw the tall man talking to a woman I hadn't noticed before. She wore a knitted cap and her face was old, lined and kindly, but within seconds it turned angry. "Well I'm not going to take it!" Her voice rose from a whisper.

The man shook his head. "You have to, Octavia! That's the reason you're here! They're coming. The ship's been spotted twice in the last few days!"

"Which is why I'm not touching it. I don't want to end up in the bottom of the Sound, as dead as a dodo. No thank you! I'll take some paintings, and that's my lot. As for the book and map, no way!"

"You have to take them. You got the short straw, so that's the deal. Time's of the essence, Octavia. The octopus is rising, the pirates have returned and now we have those blasted strangers to contend with. They've been digging everywhere. They're going to find them, I'm certain of it, and then where will we be?" He hissed something I couldn't hear and flecks of spit flew from his lips.

"We should go and dig up the chests as soon as we can. Move them to the other side of the country."

"But no one wants to risk it, not even you! Or have you changed your mind?"

"Do you realize they've been watching me?" Octavia asked. "I saw them outside my house last night. I don't know how they found out, someone must have blabbed. Probably Marge, down in her cups."

"They're watching all of us, hence why I'm holding this bazaar tonight."

"Which makes absolutely no sense... A midnight garage sale? Whoever heard of such nonsense, Montgomery? If anything it's going to attract even more attention. What were you thinking?"

Montgomery shook his head. "It was the best way I could think of to make the trade without it looking like we're trying to hide something. And I wanted to conduct it at an hour that wouldn't attract normal people."

Octavia folded her arms. "There are normal people in your house as we speak. Didn't you see that boy and his mother? They're as normal as peas and onions."

"We can get rid of them easily enough," Montgomery said. And then he raised his hand and I saw he was clutching a thick, ancient-looking old leathery book. "Now please, take it!"

"No. Give it to someone else. I'm already doing more than enough..."

I froze as the doorbell rang. The low chime reminded me of the bell I'd heard on the beach. Montgomery and Octavia rushed to the window at the end of the hall and glanced through it. "It's them! They found us!" Octavia said. She looked furious and frightened. "I told you-"

"There's no time for blame. We need to pull ourselves together and act like nothing's amiss. Quick, help me!"

"No. I'm leaving. I'm sorry, I'm no longer cut out for the Society." Octavia stumbled down the stairs leaving Montgomery frozen in the hall. Then the cat bit the back of my leg and I yelped. My hand leaped up to cover my mouth but it was too late.

The door flew open and a long shadow fell across the floor.

6

THE LIFE AND TIMES OF THE
NORTH AMERICAN TOAD

Montgomery stood before me, his eyes bulging as they bored into mine. "What the devil are you..."

"I'm sorry." I pointed at the purring cat as it wandered off. "He was hungry, so I fed him. Her. Whatever it is."

I grew more flustered as his eyes widened further. It was like they were sucking the whole world into them.

"You'll do," he said.

I didn't know what that meant and didn't want to find out. I tried to squeeze past him but he blocked my path and thrust the book at me. "Here." He pressed it into my hands. "I think you'll enjoy this. Keep it safe, yes?"

"I..."

"Keep it safe," he repeated, "and secret. In five days post it to the address on the flap inside. You'll be able to read it once five days have passed."

"Read what?"

"The address!" He said this like I should know what he meant. I didn't.

"But I..." Somehow I was now holding the book like it was

already mine. Despite its size, it was light and it had that old book smell in spades. My eyes flitted over the title; 'The Life and Times of the North American Toad.'

Montgomery dug into his pocket, pulled out his wallet and thrust twenty dollars into my hand. "For the shipping." And then he added another fifty. "This is for your troubles. Yes?" He glanced over his shoulder. The conversation downstairs had fallen silent. I hoped Mom was okay. "Will you do as I ask?"

"I guess..." What I actually wanted to do was drop the book, run, find Mom and drag her out of this crazy old house if I had to.

"Dylan?" Mom called from downstairs as if reading my thoughts.

I scampered into the hall and glanced down at her.

"I couldn't find you. Everything okay?" she asked.

She didn't see the book because I'd tucked it into the pocket of my hoody. "Sure. I was just feeding Mr..."

"Ovalhide. Montgomery Ovalhide." He gave us both a warm, fake smile.

"Mr. Ovalhide's cat." I said.

"Cyril," Montgomery said, "his name is Cyril."

That figured.

"Well, it's time to go," Mom said. She was clutching a small statue of a two-headed elephant and a collage made of glittering sand dollars. "I found some very unique things here, Mr. Ovalhide."

"I'm glad to hear it, ma'am." He smiled again, but I saw the fear in his eyes as he glanced toward me. And then, as I started down the stairs, he whispered, "Five days. Don't forget."

I nodded. I didn't care about the book, I just wanted to get out of there.

We slowed as we passed by the living room. It didn't take a

Watson, let alone a Sherlock Holmes to realize who Octavia and Montgomery had seen from the upstairs window.

A seriously weird looking man and woman stood on the far side of the room. They were rifling through a box of old maps while everyone else tried to act like they weren't watching. Somehow the couple looked even more fake and strange than the other people.

The man was small with a ratty face and sharp ratty teeth. He had a big bushy grey beard and wore a dark woolen fisherman's cap. His eyes were hidden by a pair of round black sunglasses. He smelled of stale motor oil and sawdust. The woman beside him had a ratty face too and jagged teeth. Her huge piercing green eyes were magnified by the thick glasses she wore. She flicked through the maps with thin, scrawny pencil-like fingers and slowed as she glanced up toward me. She smiled, but it wasn't nice.

Suddenly I realized that they were the people I'd seen on the beach. The ones with the shovels who'd been burying corpses, or searching for lost secrets...

The man turned my way and I felt his stare from behind the dark circles of glass. "Hello little fellow," he said gritting his teeth together.

7

X MARKS THE SPOT

"Come on, Dylan." Mom gave the man a seriously cold smile as she steered me from the room. It seemed like she'd finally realized they were bad people.

Even though I didn't look back, I could still feel the strange couple's laser-like stares burning into my spine as we hurried off into the night.

"What idiot did that?" Mom muttered as we stood in the driveway facing the dark houses lining the street. It was surprising anyone could sleep with all the traffic from the Midnight bazaar and the weirdoes wandering around in the night.

And then I saw what she was talking about.

A car had parked in front of ours, almost boxing us in. It was a low, old-fashioned sedan painted the color of rotten wood. Dents and dings dotted the fenders, and the windshield was split by a spider-web-like crack.

"Come on." Mom unlocked our car and swore under her breath as she backed out.

The relief of escaping the midnight bazaar faded as I

glanced into the mirror and saw the weird couple climbing into the old car behind us. Its lights blazed as they reversed, made a squealing juddering u-turn and followed us down the street.

Our road was only a few blocks away, but I wished it was further because they were still right behind us and I didn't want them to know where we were going.

They slowed as we veered off onto the dirt road to our house. Then they pulled over and as we drove over the rise they passed out of view. If Mom noticed them, she didn't say anything.

Dad and Jamie were still up when we got home. Dad was in the kitchen putting away the pots and pans and Jamie was playing video games. Thankfully he didn't pay any attention when I said goodnight to Mom and Dad and hurried upstairs.

I snatched the curtains shut and set the crazy old book on the desk beside my dead phone. I was anxious for the five days to pass so I could mail it off like Mr. Ovalhide had asked, anything to get rid of it. Out of curiosity, I lifted the cover and gazed at the flyleaf.

An address was scrawled inside but it was hard to read it in the dim light. I flicked through the pages and their musty smell wafted up to my nostrils.

The book didn't seem like anything I'd want to read. I was about to set it down when my finger reached the center and slipped into a hollow.

I opened the book. The middle had been carved out and inside the cavity was a battered old compass and a piece of yellowed, folded paper with a hand-drawn picture of a beach on it. A stretch of water was depicted with long wavy lines and there was a distant mountain that looked like Mount Rainier. On a stippled patch of sandy beach, right by a rock, someone had scrawled an X... like it was a treasure map!

I thought back to the couple I'd seen digging and a slow

shiver tickled down my spine as I remembered their silhouettes. I was certain they'd been the weird couple that had turned up at the midnight bazaar. The ones who had followed us home…

What had I gotten myself into?

I flipped the map over and read a strange line written in faded, spidery writing:

'Find a hard old heart half buried in the sand, five steps south dig with your hand.'

"What's that supposed to mean?" I asked.

I slept badly. My dreams were full of ghostly ships, creepy rolling fog, and strange people looming outside in the woods, staring up at my window.

IT WAS A RELIEF TO BE AWAKE THE NEXT MORNING, AT LEAST until my sleepy eyes settled on the book. "Day one," I sighed as I realized it was too soon to ship it off. A moment later my door swung open and Jamie strode in. "Do you have my spare controller?" he demanded.

"No. Why would I?"

He said nothing as his gaze swept around the room and fixed on the box perched on my chair. He rifled through it, dropped it with a clunk, and glanced at my desk. "The Life and Times of the North American Toad," he said with an exaggerated sneer. "What's this, your autobiography?" He leafed through the book with his thick meaty fingers. "You're even stranger than I thought, Dyllyboo."

"Put it down. It's rare."

"Of course it's rare. The only people who'd read garbage like this are lonely weirdos like you."

"Just leave it alone."

"Just leave it alone," he said, mimicking my voice in a stupid whiny way. As he held the book by his side, the cover opened and the map fell out onto the floor.

He hadn't noticed. Not yet.

"I'll tell you what," he said, "I'll give the book back when you return my controller. How about that?"

"I told you, I don't have it. But I'll help you look for it, if you ask nicely. *How about that?"*

Jamie slammed the book down on the desk. "You've got until ten o'clock. That's *AM.*"

"And then what happens?" I asked, trying not to look at the treasure map. It was right by his bare foot.

"What happens after that is I crush you like the worthless *toad* you are. They'll have to add a page about how you became extinct in the next edition of this stupid book."

"Fine," I said, hoping he'd leave before he noticed the map.

"Ten a.m.," he said once more like I hadn't heard the first time. He eyed the box again, rummaged through it, yawned, and strode away with the map stuck to his foot.

I jumped out of bed and followed him.

He stopped by the door and regarded me suspiciously. "What?"

I moved so close our noses were almost touching and carefully put my foot on the paper. I clapped a friendly hand on his shoulder and forced a smile. "We'll find your controller, Jamie. It's here somewhere, don't worry."

He shook his head. "You're really strange, Dyllyboo." I grabbed the map up off the floor as he returned to his room. Thankfully he hadn't damaged it with his gross, stinking feet.

I glanced at the X on the beach. What was it marking? I thought about the weird conversation between Octavia and Mr. Ovalhide. How she'd said they should dig up the chests. And his reply... but *no one wants to risk it, not even you!*

What did it mean? Did I even want to know? No. What I wanted to do was put the map back in the hollowed-out book and hide it somewhere Jamie would never look, like the bookshelf, and take it to the nearest post office in exactly five days. Just like I'd been told to do.

But I couldn't help gazing at the X again. What was buried there? Gold? Rubies? Gold *and* rubies? Would it be valuable enough for me to buy my own house, one without living Jamie in it?

Maybe I should just take a quick look... I'd never seen real life treasure before, and I doubted I'd ever get the chance again. It couldn't hurt to dig it up and take a quick peek, could it? Plus, it would make a cool story to tell Sam and Caden, if I ever found my phone charger.

I slipped the map back into the book and hid it under the mountain of dirty socks that had piled up during the move. Then I went to look for Jamie's spare controller so I could keep him off my case. I found it pretty fast; it had been in his room the whole time, sitting right under his stupid nose.

He didn't have time to play games anyway because he and Mom and Dad had planned to go for a run at a local park. So I was home alone and knowing them, they'd be gone for hours.

I played Jamie's games for a while and was careful not to save them so he wouldn't know, but I found it hard to enjoy myself.

I kept thinking about the map and the inky X scrawled on the beach.

Langley was only a mile away; maybe I could find a book in the library about the local beaches. I could be back home before Mom, Dad and Jamie if I was fast, and that way-

Thud, thud, thud.

Someone was at the door.

Who? Why? My mind leaped straight back to the weirdoes from the midnight bazaar and how they'd followed us.

I tip-toed to the door, my heart thumping like a snare drum.

8

MILLICENT CHIMES

"Millicent Chimes," said the frail old lady on the doorstep. She stood there like a vampire waiting to be invited inside. "Pleased to meet you." She offered her hand, and I shook it lightly, worried I'd crush it if I wasn't careful.

She was a tiny, bony old woman and she reminded me of a bird with her slightly hooked nose and heavily lidded eyes. She wore a dark blue bonnet, with a matching jacket and trousers and her smile was all chocolates, sunshine and roses, but her eyes worried me. They seemed to look right through me like she knew everything there was to know. "You must be the new neighbor, Mr?"

"Dylan Wilde. My mom and dad can't come to the door right now. Can I help you?"

"Maybe," she said. "Who knows?" She grinned showing tiny yellow teeth. "I just came to introduce myself. You know, to be neighborly. I live just down the road." She pointed off into the trees and when she turned back she glanced past me toward the hall. I didn't like that and closed the door a little.

"Well," I said, running out of words.

"Well, what?" Her piercing, silvery eyes fixed on mine again.

"I was on my way out. So..."

"Going anywhere interesting?"

"Just the library."

"Care for a ride?"

I shook my head. "No. Thank you. I'm going to ride my bike, so..."

"Ah, I understand." She placed a cool hand over mine. "You want to fly down the trail with the wind in your hair, the smell of cut grass in your nose. Alive and hurtling through life at a million miles per hour. I'll leave you to it, Dylan. I'm just down the way so we'll cross paths at some point or another I'm sure."

She turned and strode down the track. I watched for a second, glad that she'd gone. Then I locked the front door and grabbed my bike from the back yard.

Soon I was coasting down the hill, the wind in my hair, the smell of freshly cut grass filling my nostrils just as she'd said. It was warm and the sky was a bright sunny blue with chalky puffs of clouds. I felt good, better than I had for days.

I shot through Langley. It was crowded and there were people everywhere I looked. Most of them were tourists, which I guessed made me a local. It was a weird thought because I probably felt more like a tourist than the tourists did themselves. I cycled up the hill to the library and glanced over at the post office as I locked my bicycle in the stand. "Four days." I muttered.

The doors swung open and I smiled at the librarian as I walked in. It was a small place but they had plenty of books and most of the titles were newer than the one we'd had back home.

I wandered among the shelves of books toward the back

where the local history section was and crouched down to examine the books about Whidbey Island. I picked one about the island's wildlife.

It was a slim hardback full of illustrations of whales, seals and birds, and as I glanced at a picture of an eagle soaring over the blue water and the mountains in the distance, I realized how lucky we were to be living on the island. Then I noticed there was no references at all to bears or mountain lions, so it seemed Jamie must have made that stuff up.

My fingers slowed as I turned the next page. It was a picture of *the* beach, the one from the map! I could tell right away because Mount Rainier loomed in the background, its huge peak thick and white with snow.

As I read the caption, my finger slowed over a passage. I read and re-read it twice:

'Double Bluff beach is not only a scenic, treasured place but also the fabled haunt of the legendary pirate Captain Grimdire.'

Captain Grimdire? It had to be a joke surely?

And then I remembered the mist and the ship that had sailed past me last night. My heart began to thump as I rifled through the index, hoping to find more information about Captain Grimdire, but he was only mentioned in that one measly sentence. I leafed back to it and read it again. "Captain Grimdire," I whispered as I stood and glanced around.

A librarian was sorting the returned books and putting them back on the nearby shelves. I wanted to ask her if she knew anything about Captain Grimdire but I could hear some kids talking nearby and I suddenly felt foolish.

Maybe there was a book on local folklore and legends... I could look for it myself, no one else had to know. I turned and wandered down the next row of shelves. There; a small section on folklore. I scanned the covers with my finger until I found it:

'Hidden Whidbey's Monstrous Myths and Lofty Legends!'

Before I could slide the book out, there was a blur of motion beside me and a fast, pale freckled hand shot out and grabbed it.

"Hey!" I turned to find an annoying-looking boy beside me.

He had wild, russet hair that was even messier than mine, and his hazel eyes narrowed angrily. His freckled nose wrinkled as he spoke. "Hey what?" He looked at me but didn't let go of the book.

"I was here first." I pulled it away from him and locked it under my folded arms like it was a football.

Two more kids appeared. One was a black boy about my age with big silver framed glasses and soft thoughtful eyes. The other was a girl with the same wild hair and pale skin as the book thief. She had a pretty, kind looking face, but her brow was starting to furrow. "What's the problem, Zachary?" she asked, her voice mildly irritated.

"The problem is this goober," Zachary nodded toward me. "He snatched our book."

The girl rolled her eyes and the other boy looked embarrassed.

"Hand it over," Zachary said, "time's of the essence. We are members of a powerful, ancient order and we need that book right now." He sighed impatiently as he held his hand out.

"Ancient order?" the girl asked. "You only started this stupid club two weeks ago, and I still can't figure out why I agreed to join."

Zachary faked a smile. "You joined, Emily because without us you'd be nothing more than a lone wolf. All. Summer. Long. Or should I say, lone chihuahua?" He turned back to me. "Her friends are all on vacation and she couldn't go with them. That's why her eyes are so red. She's probably cried enough tears to fill two swimming pools." Emily's eyes weren't red at all. "What about you?" Zachary rounded on me, "Why are you hanging out on your own? Are you some kind of weirdo?"

"I just moved here," I sneered, defending myself.

"Right," he said, "in that case, you definitely have to give us the book."

"Why?" I clutched it tight expecting he'd try to grab it. He looked like a grabber.

"Because we've lived here longer than you. That means we have seniority." Zachary said. The other boy rolled his eyes and gave me an apologetic shrug. "I bet you don't even have a library card," Zachary continued, "do you?"

Emily sighed and smiled at me. "I'm sure..." she paused, "what's your name?"

"Dylan."

"Dylan, I'm Emily," she said, "this is Jacob, and you've already met my brother Zach. Would you let us have a quick look at the book, and then we'll give it right back?"

"Of course," I said. She and Jacob seemed nice. Zach on the other hand...

The librarian started wheeling a book cart down our aisle so we moved toward the tables at the front of the library. "What are you looking for anyway?" I asked as I handed Emily the book. Zach peered out the window. I didn't know if he was being moody or just strange. Either seemed likely.

"We're looking for a pirate," Jacob said matter of factly. He had a calm, soft voice, the opposite of Zach's. I wanted to tell him I was too but kept quiet. The situation was getting seriously weird.

"Jeez, you didn't need to go and blab about it, Jacob!" Zach said. And then his eyes narrowed as he continued to gaze through the window. "Oh wow, we've got some new ones."

"New what?" Emily asked as she leafed through the book's index.

"New weirdos," Zach said. "Who wears a coat like that in summer?"

I moved to the window and peered out. It was the couple from the midnight bazaar. They were across the street, glancing around as if they were searching for something. "Oh... It's them," I said, without meaning to.

And then the pair of them peered toward the library as if they'd heard me.

9

THE STRANGERS

"Who are they?" Zach asked, his eyes narrowing as they flitted over mine. Jacob adjusted his glasses, peered through the window, then turned and strode away.

I ducked back as the strangers glanced my way again. "I don't know them, not personally," I said. "I've just seen them around and I'm pretty sure they're bad news. I don't want them to see me."

"Let's wait here until they're gone," Emily said. And then she shook her head. "Oh great, they're coming this way!"

"Here you go." Jacob appeared at my side and handed me a huge baking book with a big gooey green cake on the cover.

"What's this for?" I asked.

"Cover your face with it when you walk out," he said. "So they can't see you."

It was a pretty good plan, and I didn't have a better one. "Thanks. But my bike's outside and I need it."

"Which one is it?" Emily asked.

"The red mountain bike, it's locked up" I said.

"Give me the key. We'll meet you in the park at the bottom of the hill," Emily said.

"Thanks." I handed her the key, opened the book to the center and held it over my face as the doors slid open.

I could hear the woman's strange coat rustle across the carpet as she passed, then I saw the peak of the man's blue fisherman's cap as I walked carefully down the stairs. I tensed, half expecting a hand to grab a hold of my shoulder at any moment.

I walked down the sidewalk, lowering the book as I glanced back. I could see Jacob and Zach, then I spotted Emily behind them, wheeling my bike down the hill. There was no sign of the strangers but I watched as each of the kids peeled off down a different alleyway, presumably to throw off anyone observing them.

The park where we were meeting up was little more than a small square of grass surrounded by flowers and a picnic table beneath a rustic metal roof. It made good cover and I quickly ducked under it and sat down to wait on one of the benches. Soon the others joined me. Emily tossed me my keys, and I caught them one-handed, which was a relief because they nearly went flying out of my fingers.

"So you guys never saw those people before?" I asked.

"Nope," Zach said. "They're new. This island's definitely chock full of weirdoes but I'd have noticed those two. I keep track of nutters like that in a notebook. I call it my list of lunatics."

I wondered if he'd included himself in his list. "So," I asked, trying to sound casual, "you said you were looking for a pirate." I glanced at the book in Jacob's hand. I was glad he had it, it was better than Zach at least.

"Not here," Zach said, "the walls have ears."

"What about the flowers, do they have ears too?" Emily teased as slow heavy bees droned from blossom to blossom.

"Shut up," Zach said, "you've already said too much." He gave me a slow, suspicious glare.

"Fine," Emily said, "I'm starving. Are you hungry, Jacob?"

He nodded. "I only ate a single slice of cheese for breakfast."

"What about you, Dylan?" she asked.

I nodded, realizing I actually was pretty hungry, now that she'd mentioned it.

"Let's go to our house," Emily said, "we can get something to eat, have a look at the book and then Dylan can take it home with him."

Zach folded his arms across his chest. "I don't want him knowing where we live. He might be a spy."

"For who?" Jacob sounded genuinely curious.

"Who knows," Zach said, narrowing his eyes. "The world's full of agents of chaos. And their moles."

"Moles of chaos?" Emily laughed and turned back to me. "Are you a spy, Dylan?"

I shook my head. "I don't think so."

"Good, let's go then." Emily led the way.

I realized I really liked them as we walked up the hill. Well, two of them at least. Jacob was smart and easy going. Emily was kind, except when she got impatient with her brother, but he was pretty annoying. I noticed that she called him Zach but as soon as he got on her nerves it changed to Zachary.

Zach... Zach was downright suspicious, but he got a little friendlier. Although I did catch him eyeballing my clothes, my bicycle, even my hair, as if searching for clues.

They lived in a big old house at the edge of town. Inside it was cool and full of dark furniture and more books than I'd ever seen. Jacob and Emily made sandwiches and Zach filled glasses with ice and orange juice. "I suppose we're going to have to show him the Towering Lair of Eternal Secrets," he said.

"What's the Towering Lair of Eternal Secrets?" I asked.

A moment later I found out. The Towering Lair of Eternal Secrets was a tree house at the back of their wild, overgrown yard. Someone had built a dumb waiter on the outside. Zach scampered up the ladder like a squirrel, pulled a lever and the tray with our drinks and food slowly rose into the air. Jacob climbed up next, clutching the book, and then it was Emily's turn.

I couldn't help but grin as I followed them. It was pretty neat, and I realized I'd never been in a tree house before.

We ate our food and Zach talked a lot, in between chugging his drink and burping.

He was full of *facts*, and I didn't believe any of them, although I was sure he did. By the time I'd finished my sandwich, he'd told me that cats couldn't see water, and that was why they drank milk. That the world was hollow and full of giants and earthquakes were them banging their fists against the inside of the planet because they wanted to get out. Then he told me bats can talk but that they only speak Romanian, and he was totally serious.

I was coming to the conclusion that he was an idiot, but he made me laugh. Now and then he had a knowing look in his eyes, like even he thought some of the stuff he was saying was crazy. Emily ignored him as she leafed through the book. A moment later her face fell. "It's gone!"

"What's gone?" Jacob pushed up his glasses as he glanced over her shoulder.

"The page about Grimdire." Emily leafed back through to the beginning. "See, there, the Legend of Captain Grimdire, page forty-three." She flicked to the middle of the book and tapped her finger on the page. "It's not there. Someone's torn it out."

"They did a good job," Zach said, tracing a finger along the fold between the pages. "There's no rips or tears. They must be experts."

"Expert what?" I asked.

"Expert page tearers," he said. "It's a thing." He paused. "Probably."

"That's weird," I said, "why would anyone do that?"

"Because they don't want anyone to know about Grimdire," Zach said, as if that should have been obvious.

"There's nothing online about him either," Jacob said, thumbing through a browser on his phone.

"How old's the book?" Emily asked.

"It was published in 1972," Zach answered. "And it definitely had the legend of Grimdire in it. I know because I've borrowed it at least a thousand times by now."

"Then you can tell us the legend," I said, "you must be able to remember it."

"Not really. There's about a hundred different stories in there. All I remember is Grimdire's really tall, wears a crumpled tricorn hat, and he always walks about in the mist." Zach paused and studied me closely. "Why are you so anxious to know about him anyway?"

They all turned toward me as they waited for a reply.

I swallowed. What could I say without sounding like I was totally nuts?

Nothing.

10

THE CURSED CAPTAIN

The words stuck in my throat. I wanted to tell them everything, but I was sure they wouldn't believe that I'd seen a giant octopus, let alone that ghostly ship. Because as I thought about it even I realized how crazy it sounded.

They might believe the treasure map though. *If* I showed it to them....

No way. It was mine, I'd found it and it was no one else's business. "I was just browsing for something to read," I lied. "Why were you guys looking for the book? It seemed important to you."

"I..." Jacob licked his lips nervously. "I saw an old ship this morning. Well, part of it. Mostly just the mast because the thing was shrouded in heavy fog."

"On a summer's day," Zach added, his eyes glinting, "and the fog wasn't anywhere else, just around the ship."

"Yeah, the mist definitely seemed to be following it," Jacob said.

"Just like the legend of Captain Grimdire!" Zach gazed into the distance as if trying to remember something.

I felt bad for holding out on them, but it was too late. Jacob had already told his story about the ship and it felt like if I mentioned it too, it would look like I was copying him. "You keep the book," I said, "it might jog your memory."

Emily grinned at me. "I'm glad we met you today, Dylan. And that you moved to the island."

That made me feel even worse, and it seemed like I had to share something at least, so I told them about the garage sale and the strangers. They listened in silence, but when I finished I felt like they knew there was more to it than I was letting on.

"Why'd this Mr. Ovalhide give you a boring book about North American Toads like it was the most important thing in the world?" Zach asked.

I shrugged.

"That doesn't make any sense," he said, and then his eyes lit up again. "Unless there was a clue hidden inside it, a secret code or something. Can you show it to us?"

"Maybe," I said.

"Maybe," Zach echoed, and the shine in his eyes dimmed. "You sure like keeping secrets, don't you?"

"Zachary!" Emily said.

"But it's true." He jumped out of the hammock. "This jerk's holding out on us. I know it, and he knows it."

"Hey Zach, chill out." Jacob gave me an awkward smile.

"I've got to go anyways," I said. Not that I wanted to. Just that morning I'd worried I'd be friendless on this island for the rest of my life, that I'd die on my lonesome below the trees with a gnarly grey beard, my only companion a rancid old goat. It was a relief to have met some potential friends, but it was looking like I'd messed it up. Again, just like I always did. "I'll see you around," I said and took the book even though I'd said they could keep it. It was doubtful I'd see them again, which meant I should probably take it back to the library. Actually, I wasn't even sure if any of us had officially checked it out.

"Come by any time," Emily said.

"Yeah," Jacob added, "it was good to meet you."

"Later, Dylan," Zach mumbled, refusing to look me in the eye.

I climbed down the ladder and stood watching the bees buzzing around the foxgloves. I thought about climbing right back up and telling them the truth, but it seemed like it was too late for that.

So I grabbed my bike and cycled away. I wasn't ready to go home, so I took a detour into Langley and peddled down First Street which took all of a few seconds. Then I slowed as I spotted a seriously steep slope leading to a beach.

I flew down it and hit the brakes when I reached the end. A meandering couple jumped as they heard my bicycle's tortured metal squeal.

The sea was calm and blue. People strolled along the pebbled shoreline and dogs ran in circles across the sand. I walked my bike toward a trail in the shelter of the bluff. Trees and bushes rustled in the cool breeze sweeping up from the water. I found a quiet spot, sat cross-legged on the grass, and began to leaf through 'Hidden Whidbey's Monstrous Myths and Lofty Legends!' as the seagulls soared above me.

The author page had a picture of a young woman with wild coppery hair. The photo had faded with time but her mischievous eyes still seemed to sparkle as she peered back at me. The introduction explained that the legends in the book were from the Pacific Northwest, but most were focused on Whidbey Island itself.

There were tales of vampires, Sasquatch, fairies and creatures called selkies. Even aliens. I skim-read the first couple of chapters. One was about a strange tribe of half man-half wolf beasts that roamed the Olympic mountains, another was about a wicked spirit that haunted forests and stole children. That one scared me, so I decided to finish the rest later, or maybe not at all.

And then I felt someone watching me.

I glanced around, expecting to find some suspicious little kid staring at me, which happened a lot, but there was no one there. The only people I could see were down at the other end of the beach.

The wind whispered through the brush beneath the bluff, drawing my attention.

Someone lurked in the shade of the trees. A man with a parrot perched on his shoulder. At least it looked like a parrot. And then I saw two more men beside him in the gloom, digging into the soil just like the strange couple had been doing the night before.

The passing clouds shifted, the sun broke through and as its rays hit them, the men faded in the light like an old movie projected onto a screen. "This is too weird." I grabbed the book, jumped up, and wheeled my bike away.

When I glanced back, the figures were completely gone.

I cycled back through town and was almost at our road when I heard something that sounded like a mechanical shark with a seriously sore throat.

The old car, the one that had followed us from the midnight bazaar, was rumbling along behind me. Clouds of grey-black smoke sputtered around it, reminding me of the pirate ship in the fog.

I glanced through the filthy windshield. The woman in the beret was driving and the man in the fisherman's cap sat in the passenger seat pointing at me and staring me in the eye like he was saying I *know*. What he knew I had no idea, but what *I* knew was that I wanted to be as far away from them as possible.

I raced up the hill. They followed faster, a billowing trail of thick dust rising up behind them amid the smoke. I cycled harder, the bike juddering from side to side as I topped the slope.

Boom. Sputter. Chang!

I glanced back. Their car had broken down. They scowled as they climbed out into the filthy cloud. I didn't feel relief, I felt terrified.

They'd followed us before. They knew where I lived or had a good idea at least. There were only a few houses on our road...

And then, as if I wasn't worried enough, the shadow of a huge bird passed over me and swooped along the gravel of our driveway. The silhouette itself was oddly faded, but it was clearly the shape of a parrot.

When I looked up, there was nothing there.

11

TERRIBLE, GHOSTLY THINGS

Mom and Dad were home when I rushed through the front door. I joined them in the living room and played a few games, trying to get the parrot and strangers off my mind.

Jamie skulked in the corner, swiping through his phone and gazing up at the TV, pointing out every single mistake I made. I didn't care; playing games was helping me forget my problems, for a while at least.

Later, I went up to my room, flopped onto my bed and studied the map. Daydreams of digging up the treasure filled my thoughts. Slowly dusk turned to night and finally, I rolled over and fell asleep.

IT WAS DARK WHEN I WOKE AND THE CURTAINS WERE A rectangle of black. I reached for the glass on the bedside table and then realized there was no bedside table. I was in my new room, and there was no glass either.

Shadows filled the hallway, but I was too tired to care. My

mouth was bone dry and I needed a drink. I slipped quietly down the stairs.

Wilson climbed up from his bed, circled my legs, and was almost back on his cushion when his ears rose high and he stared at the front door.

"What is it?" I whispered.

Something rattled outside. I thought about calling for Mom and Dad, but what if it was just a raccoon or chipmunk? I'd never live it down, especially if Jamie found out.

Slowly, carefully, I drew back the living room curtain. My heart thumped hard.

A man stood on the dirt road. He was watching the house.

Wilson growled and slunk away.

I stared out the window, unable to move. It looked like he hadn't seen me as he continued to gaze up at the roof. Then something soared down through the darkness and landed on his shoulder.

It was the parrot!

As my eyes adjusted to the gloom, I saw the man's baggy leggings, long dirty-white shirt and the golden earring gleaming in the moonlight.

"The pirate!" I croaked, remembering him from the beach.

Then I spotted the cutlass clenched in his hand.

My scream caught in my throat. I was about to race upstairs and wake Mom and Dad when he strode toward the front door all jerky and strange, like a clip from an old-fashioned movie.

The security lights flickered and a dim yellow glow lit the porch. He raised his cutlass over his eyes as if the light was somehow blinding him and stumbled back.

Glowing holes appeared on his clothes where the light had fallen. Suddenly he grew *thinner*, his form fading away like he was a ghost.

The parrot squawked as the man nimbly jumped into the shadows. Wilson leaped up and started growling and barking. The bird's startled call seemed to annoy him more than the creepy pirate right outside our house. Bozo!

"Get him!" I said, opening the door. Wilson flew out and scurried across the porch, his hackles rising.

The pirate fled toward the trees and melted into the darkness. Soon there was no sign of him but Wilson stood growling near the tree line, his tail pointing in the air, his body unusually alert.

"Dylan?"

I jumped a mile high as Dad bounded into the living room. He had an umbrella clenched in his hand as if it was a baseball bat and a phone in the other with 911 on the screen. His finger hovered over the call button. "Is someone out there?"

I almost said yes. Almost. But then what? Tell him there was a pirate ghost lurking in the woods with a dead parrot on his shoulder? No one would believe that! Not even Dad, no matter how much he loved me. My life would become an even bigger mockery than it already was. "Uh, I think it was a raccoon, maybe," I said. "Wilson!" I called. He scurried over and leaped up the steps, looking relieved to be back. I couldn't blame him.

Dad put the umbrella down, slipped his phone into his dressing gown pocket and shut the door. "Why are you up?" he whispered.

"I was getting a drink of water. Then Wilson freaked out."

"Okay. Well, you look pretty freaked out yourself. Next time there's a problem you come and get me, okay?"

"Sure." I grabbed the water, patted Wilson's head, and went back to bed.

I lay there, my eyes glued to the crack in the drapes. I half expected the ghostly pirate's face to appear at any moment, or to hear the ragged parrot tapping its beak upon the glass.

Finally, I forced myself to leap up and snatch the curtains together. I stayed awake for forever, my mind turning, my thoughts spinning.

What was happening? The midnight bazaar, the treasure map, the library book with the missing page. The strangers... the pirates.

When I finally fell asleep, I dreamed about terrible, ghostly things.

12

THE EMPTY HOUSE

My head felt like it was full of mud the next morning, and my eyes were sore and tired. I opened the curtains and gazed into the trees. There was nothing out there, no shady pirate or ratty old ghost parrot perched in the branches. Not a single scrap of evidence to suggest that the whole moonlight freakfest had been anything other than my messed up imagination.

But it *had* happened, I knew it. And I needed help, big time. The only people I could think of who might even begin to believe me were Jacob, Emily and Zach, which meant I needed to find them and tell them everything I knew.

But what if they didn't believe me either?

"They will," I whispered. They had to.

I showered and had toast with blackberry jam for breakfast. Dad was in the living room rearranging all his books so that they were in alphabetical order. He looked a little embarrassed when I noticed what he was doing. "Is it okay if I go out with my friends?" I asked.

"What?"

I told him about Jacob, Emily and Zach.

"You've already made new friends?" He seemed pleased. "That's awesome, Dylan. I told you this was going to be a good move!"

I didn't necessarily agree with that but didn't want to interrupt him as he dug into his wallet and handed me ten dollars. "This is lunch money," he said with a serious look. "Make sure you're home by six. And take your phone."

"My phone's dead, remember?"

"Right. Well, take mine then, just in case." He handed me his phone.

"Thanks." I stuffed a bottle of water into my backpack along with 'Hidden Whidbey's Monstrous Myths and Lofty Legends!' and the North American Toad book before heading out on my bike.

It was bright, sunny and warm. White tents had sprung up on the edge of the field outside of town to sell fireworks for the Fourth of July and car after car slowly meandered by. It seemed like a nice normal day, like nothing shady or strange could possibly be going on. And while a big part of me wished I could join everyone else in their happy blind ignorance, a larger, newer part of me felt excited. Things were happening. Epic things. And I had friends that understood that, or so I hoped.

I parked my bike on the lawn outside Zach and Emily's house and knocked on their door. There were no cars in their driveway, and I wondered if they were even home.

A moment later the door opened and a girl glanced down at me. She was wearing a lot of makeup and her hair was the same color as Emily's. In fact, she looked just like Emily, except taller and older. She was definitely in high school.

"Yeah?" She had a phone plastered to her ear so I didn't know if she was talking to me or not.

"Hi," I said.

She looked at me as if she hadn't quite decided what I was. "Hold on, honey."

"Me?" I asked.

"What do you want?" she asked, pulling the phone from her ear. Then I realized she hadn't been talking to me at all.

My burning cheeks must have been beet red. "Is-"

"Dylan!" Emily walked into the hall and stopped, a bowl of cereal in her hand. She glanced at the girl. "Let him in, Violet."

Violet gave me another wary glance, clamped the phone back to her head and wandered off, gabbing.

Moments later Emily and I climbed the ladder to the tree house to look for Zach. He was perched on a pile of cushions in the corner, reading a book about werewolves. He glanced up and gave me a suspicious look, one he seemed to have inherited from Violet. "What are you doing here?" he asked as he set the book down.

"Zachary!" Emily said.

"What?"

"Don't talk to Dylan like that. He's our friend."

"He is? I don't remember agreeing to that. Are you and Jacob the bosses of everything now?"

"Look," I said, my cheeks flushing bright red again as Emily placed a soft hand on my arm. "I'm sorry about yesterday. You were right, I didn't tell you everything. And... some really weird things happened after I left here. I need help."

"Things?" Zach raised an eyebrow.

"There was this parrot, and-"

"Stop!" Zach held his hand up. "Wait until Jacob's here." He checked his phone. "He's due in nine minutes."

"Fine," I agreed, shocked that he didn't want to know the whole story instantly.

Emily shrugged, grabbed a glass of juice from the dusty shelf and flopped down into a beanbag chair.

Not even a minute passed before Zach looked at his phone again, sighed loudly and said, "Just give us a hint."

"Zachary!" Emily rolled her eyes.

"What? There's still eight minutes to go, and what if he's late?" Zach said. "We're just supposed to sit here all day doing nothing? I just want to know if his story's worth all the hype."

So I told them about the pirates and the parrot on the beach.

"Whoa, interesting," Zach said, and gave his phone an irritable glance, like the existence of time itself was there just to annoy him. "Tell us a bit more. Jacob won't be here for ages."

He did this until I'd told them everything, then when Jacob turned up a few minutes later I had to tell them the whole story again.

"Did you bring the map with you?" Jacob asked as he studied me closely.

"Yeah," I replied, even though part of me still wanted to keep it to myself. I took the book from my bag and set it down.

"The Life and Times of the American Toad," Zach read, "wow that sounds like the most boring book that was ever written. What a snoozefest!"

"That's exactly why they used it," I said as I opened it up and revealed the map hidden inside.

I carefully unfolded it and handed it to Jacob. Zach and Emily crowded in behind him.

"That's Double Bluff beach!" Emily said as she pointed at the map "This has to be Mount Rainier across the water."

"Then where's Seattle?" Zach asked.

"It probably didn't exist when this map was made," Jacob said.

"Wow, it must be *super* old!" Zach said as he snatched it and sniffed the page. "It's got that old book smell! Can I have it?"

"No, I need to mail it back with the book," I told him.

"Can I see the book?" Emily asked. I slowly handed it to her. She opened the cover and tried to make out the address. "Can you actually read this?"

"No," I said, "I know this going to sound crazy but-"

"Yeah, sure, crazier than zombie parrots and ghost pirates." Zach added, but he smiled to show he was joking.

"Maybe." I returned his grin. It still felt weird telling them everything, but I wasn't as nervous as I'd been at first. "What I was going to say is, the address isn't supposed to be readable until it's time to ship the book. Does that make sense?"

"Scientifically, no," Jacob said, "but for Whidbey Island, yes."

"My brother calls it Weirdbey Island" I added.

"Whoa, nice! This place totally is Weirdbey Island!" Zach laughed and slapped the top of his leg. Then he looked each of us in the eye one by one "Now, who's ready to dig up some treasure?"

"What if it's cursed?" I asked. It was possible. *Anything* was possible.

"Yeah, there is that," Jacob added. "I don't want to die of some ancient magical disease."

"Like your flesh slipping from your bones!" Zach said. "Or your eyes falling out and worms slithering from your nostrils and your tongue turning-"

"Maybe we should go back to the place where you got the map," Emily said, " and talk to the people who gave it to you. Maybe they could tell us more about it." She grabbed Zach's phone and took a picture of the map. "Just in case they ask for it back…"

I glanced out the crooked window. It was midmorning. Surely the house couldn't actually be as creepy as it had seemed in the middle of the night? Not in broad daylight. "Okay."

We climbed down to the yard and Emily and Zach ran to their garage. By the time they wheeled their bikes out, Jacob was already perched on his silver and purple mountain bike, which he'd parked on the grass next to mine.

We cycled through town. The breeze was cool against my arms and face as the world flew by in shades of green and gold. The sky was huge and blue and seemed to go on forever. We had to double back a few times before I remembered exactly which street it was but we soon found it. Lawn sprinklers whispered and hissed, dogs barked, and a gang of little kids ran alongside us trying to soak us with their squirt guns. Zach hollered and swerved at them and they scattered like a flock of starlings as they vanished into the landscaped yards.

We all hit our brakes with a squeal as we reached the end of the street and I pointed to the house.

It looked abandoned. There were no cars in the cracked, potholed driveway and the bushes seemed wilder and more overgrown than I remembered. High above them, the branches of the trees closed in, casting heavy shadows on the worn sagging rooftop. The porch was mat-less and desolate, the windows dark. Even the curtains were gone.

It was like no one had lived there in years.

❧ 13 ❧

HIDDEN LANE

"**I** don't get it," I said as I stood there gripping my handlebars. I'd only been there two nights ago... how had he emptied the place out so fast? And where had Mr. Ovalhide gone?

I turned to find the others watching me from their bikes.

Jacob looked confused, Emily looked baffled and I couldn't tell what Zach was thinking as he studied me. Were they about to cycle away? "I didn't make it up," I said. "The house was full of weird old junk and there were loads of people too, I swear."

I marched up to the porch and gazed through the window. There was no two ways about it, everything from the paintings to the carpets to the furniture was gone.

"I believe you." Zach nodded. "I don't see why you'd make it up. Not unless you're totally nuts. I guess that's possible, you do look kinda crazy."

"I believe you too." Jacob said, "I know when people are full of–"

"I wonder where they went?" Emily asked, cutting over him.

"I don't know," I shrugged, feeling a bit better after they'd said they believed me. It wasn't just my mystery to solve; now it belonged to all of us.

"We should go to Double Bluff," Zach said, "and dig up the treasure."

"We don't know for sure that it is treasure, Zachary," Emily said. "They could have buried anything there. It might even be a trap."

"A trap?" I hadn't thought of that. Suddenly the day didn't seem so bright.

"Emily's right," Jacob said with a long, thoughtful look, "they could have hidden anything there."

"Yeah, including a megaton of gold and diamonds," Zach said. "But we won't know if we don't look."

Jacob shook his head. "I think we need to do some more research, find out what we're up against first."

"You always say that." Zach gave an irritable snort.

"Because it makes sense," Jacob replied, "First a ghost ship, then pirates...then a weirdo shoves an old book into Dylan's hands and he gets followed twice by those strangers."

"Don't forget the giant octopus," I added.

"Yeah," Jacob agreed, nodding sagely, "and then there's Captain Grimdire and those missing pages. We need to find out what's going on before we dig up anything."

"Exactly," Emily said.

"Two against two, right?" Zach looked at me wide eyed, waiting for my vote.

I wanted to find the treasure as much as he did, but the thought of a trap worried me. "I think we should try and find out more about this first, if we can."

"Come on!" Zach said, but as he looked from me to Emily and then to Jacob, his shoulders shrank and he seemed to grow a little smaller. "Right. No treasure for us today. No doubloons, no emeralds. No gold bars big enough to buy all the books and ice cream in the world. So how are we supposed to research Grimdire? I've already looked online and there was zilch. I've even asked grandpa, and he's lived here longer than anyone else I know and he's never heard of him either..."

"What about the author that wrote the book of legends?" Jacob asked.

"Gillian Tweedle?" Emily said.

"Yeah." Jacob tapped his phone screen. I'd never seen anyone type so fast. "Gillian Tweedle... Bingo! Apparently, she lives on Hidden Lane in Freeland where she runs a cat rescue place. And Hidden Lane is..." another flurry of fingers, "not that far. We could get the next bus..." his fingers flew across the screen again, "which is due in just under forty-seven minutes and thirty five seconds."

"Let's go," Zach called as he sped away.

It was early afternoon by the time we got to Freeland and the bus was so hot it felt like we'd been riding in a baked potato. The roasting sun blazed through the windows, the trees lining the road seemed to glow and the asphalt shimmered as we leaped down the steps and pulled our bikes off the rack on the front of the bus.

Jacob checked his phone for directions and then we were off, racing down a curvy lane, shooting past houses, our spinning wheels whirring in unison.

It turned out Hidden Lane was well named. We took a right halfway down a long road that seemed to stretch on for forever. According to Zach, it had been built by the Romans, which made no sense. Then, after doubling back, we turned onto a heavily wooded street that led to Hidden Lane.

Up and down we rode, the sun blazing between the

branches until Emily spotted an ancient mossy sign and a path I was fairly sure hadn't been there the first time we'd passed by.

We followed a long twisting trail. At the end, there was a house set back among the trees. It was a faded old building, its walls creeping with ivy. On one side of the long driveway there was a teepee and on the other, there was a small wooden shed called 'The Cattery' and right in the middle of the two was a car crammed full of cardboard boxes.

"Go on, knock," Zach said as I neared the front door. It was ajar, and despite the calm air of peacefulness surrounding the place, I felt like grabbing my bike and cycling away.

Then Emily reached past me and rapped her knuckles on the door. "Hello?"

There was a clatter and rumble as something fell to the floor. And then I heard a long sigh followed by the sound of bare feet padding on wood.

The door swung open, and a woman stood before us wielding a flashlight in each hand. She shone them at each of us in turn, her eyes wide and wild. Her red hair was peppered with grey and it stood up in all directions, as if she'd just stepped out of a howling windstorm. She also looked like she hadn't slept for days. I barely recognized her as the same woman from the picture in the back of the book.

"What do you want?" she asked as she glanced behind us. And then she shone her flashlights into our eyes and demanded, "Are you even real?"

❧ 14 ❧

THE SOCIETY OF THE OWL
AND WOLF

"Of course we're real," Zach said. He shielded his face as Gillian Tweedle's flashlight blazed directly into his eyes. "And we've got questions."

"If you don't mind answering a few of them for us," Emily added.

"We borrowed your book from the library," Jacob explained.

"Again," Zach said, "I'm a fan. I've read it at least seven hundred times." He beamed a smile at her.

"My book…" she looked puzzled, "oh, that old thing. That was a long time ago. What about it?"

She seemed confused, but I was sure she knew exactly why we were there. "There's a page missing," I said, "and we want to know what it said."

"A page missing? Well, there's not much I can do about that. The publishers went out of business in the eighties and the book's been out of print ever since. Now," she glanced into the woods behind us again, "I have a great deal to do before the day's over. Before…" her eyes widened, "nightfall."

"Are you going somewhere?" Emily asked, gesturing to the boxes packed in the car.

"I'm leaving the island, for good. Me and my cats. Now," she stepped back inside the house and began to close the door, "I'll wish you a nice-"

"We want to know about Captain Grimdire!" Zach spluttered.

Gillian's eyes widened even further. "I... he doesn't... I can't..."

"We *really* need to know about him," Emily said.

"Have you... have you seen him?" Gillian whispered.

"Dylan and I saw his ship and he's seen pirates too, haven't you?" Jacob said as he looked at me.

"Yes, on the ship's deck," I said, "then on the beach. And another one last night. In the yard, right outside my house."

Gillian's fingers tightened on the door frame. She shook her head. "It *is* happening again. I feared it was and hoped it wasn't."

"What does that mean?" Zach asked.

She ignored him as she fixed her frightened gaze on me. "Was the man on the ship tall and wide? Did he have a long beard and tricorn hat? Did he clatter when he moved? Did his dead eyes bore into yours and suck all the light from the world?"

"Erm, no," I said. "I only saw his silhouette really."

"Then count yourself blessed."

"Who is he?" Jacob asked.

"You'd be wise not to ask that question. You'd be even wiser to go home this very instant and while away your summer in blissful ignorance," Gillian said.

"No way," Zach said, "we're already up to our neck in this. Dylan," he nodded to me, "is being stalked by pirates and who knows what else. This is *serious*. And now, there're these strangers foll-"

Gillian Tweedle sighed. "Come in. Quickly!"

She led us through the house. There were boxes everywhere, just like our house; only most were packed rather than empty. "Sit on whatever you find." She nodded toward a large living room. The furniture was gone but there were still a few crates on the floor so we sat and waited for her.

Moments later she returned with a big icy jug of lemonade and a stack of plastic cups. She filled them one by one and handed them out. The lemonade was sweet, sour and deliciously cold. I guzzled half the cup down in one shot.

"So where are you going?" Emily asked.

"To live with my sister in Chattanooga. It's about as far from this cursed island as I can get." She looked at each of us and I could see she was thinking carefully. "Time moves in circles," she said. "You were here before, or other *yous* were. And now they're old and frail and you're here, young and filled with urgency. But if I were you, I'd get out while you can."

"I just got here," I said.

"Then you have my commiserations. Whidbey Island's picture perfect. It's beautiful and magical, but there's a dark forgotten history here too. A hidden dimension that most folk never stumble into. Gerald, my husband, knew all about that. He was a member of the Society of the Owl and Wolf."

"Who are they?" Zach asked.

"Currently, whilst they still draw breath, they're a group of friends that came together just as you have. And at right about your age, strangely enough. This was a long time ago, back in the 1950s. They protected the island as did their parents before them."

"From what?" I asked, half wishing I hadn't. Did I really want to know? Did I really want to get involved?

"From all sorts of things." Gillian smiled, but it wasn't a happy smile. "The things that lurk in the shadows, out of sight. Terrible, wondrous things. Things like Captain Grimdire and his cursed crew."

"The Society..." I said, thinking back to Montgomery and Octavia. "Do they still protect the island?"

"They try. But they're old, just as I am. It's no laughing matter hunting vampires at our age, believe me."

"Vampires? Here?" I asked. It seemed Jamie hadn't been making it up after all, at least not all on his own.

"Oh, there's *all* sorts. Gerald was deep in the fray so of course I heard everything. At least until I wrote that silly old book. The Society was furious about that; they didn't want the secrets getting out. But I thought people had a right to know the truth, and I still do. After my book was published, the Society kicked Gerald out but I think he was relieved." She broke off as a sad smile twisted her lips.

"What happened?" Emily asked, her voice soft and low.

"We had thirty wonderful, blissful years where nothing happened. And then..." She paused as she took a heavy swig of lemonade. "And then it all started up again. Gerald got himself involved of course, and that was the end of him. I... I can't talk about it. I'm only telling you this so you understand what you're getting yourselves into."

"We don't necessarily want to get into anything," Jacob said.

"Then you're wise beyond your years. But still, you've come seeking answers," Gillian said, "which implies you *are* going to get involved." She gazed at Zach. "And I can see you're not going to let it go, are you?"

"We can't." Zach nodded to me. "We need to help Dylan, plus-"

"These strangers... has the man got a big fake beard?"

Gillian asked, "and the woman, does she wear a long coat even in summer?"

"Yes! That's them," I said.

"They've been on the island for weeks, digging hither and yon, menacing the locals for information. I fear they've been partially successful."

"Who are they?" Emily asked.

"I don't have the faintest idea," Gillian said, "but I know what they're looking for."

"What?" I asked.

Her forehead wrinkled up like a spider's web. "The Rotten Blight."

"The what?" Zach asked.

"Captain Grimdire's galleon." Gillian studied us again. "And now you'll want me to tell you about that too, I suppose?"

The others nodded, so I did too, even though I mostly wanted to get back into the summer light and forget about it all while I still could.

"Then I'll tell you," Gillian said, "because you must know what you're up against. But I warn you; it's a sinister, wretched tale, and what you're about to hear could change everything, forever."

We drew in close as she sat back and began.

15

FAR, FAR AWAY

"It all started far, far away in a small seaside village called Clevedon in the south west of England," Gillian began. "Each one of us must grow up somewhere and that's the place Grimdire terrorized from the age of five to fifteen. He robbed, stole, vandalized and extorted; he was a blight on everything he touched but he was far too clever to ever get caught red handed.

Fearing he'd graduate from petty crime to something far more sinister, his mother went to the authorities and they presented Grimdire with a choice; sail off with the navy, or face jail. He chose the former, and thus his seafaring life began."

Gillian paused and her brow furrowed as she checked the windows. And then she found her thread again.

"Within a year, Grimdire learned everything there was to know about sailing. Steering, trimming the sails, dropping anchor, navigating by the stars; everything.

And once he'd mastered his craft he began to work on his fellow sailors, sowing seeds of distrust in their minds, cultivating the first dark shoots of mutiny. It didn't take long for the sailors to realize that they were indeed hard done by and that if they followed Grimdire they'd double the meager wages they were paid.

Once he had the crew under his spell, Grimdire arrested the captain on his own ship and made him walk the plank. Off he went, toppling into the heaving waves, never to be seen again.

That was the day he became Captain Grimdire, a name he gave himself. Within a year, Grimdire and his men became the most feared pirates in the region. At first, they'd flag down ships under the pretense of needing urgent assistance, and then they'd seize the unsuspecting vessels. Gradually they built up their arsenal with confiscated weapons and ammunition until they had enough cannons and gunpowder to take down a small island.

Soon, Grimdire inspired such overwhelming terror that no one dared speak his name, let alone write about his filthy deeds, for fear he'd come looking for them. This is why you won't find many accounts of him, save from the few brave, or should I say foolish souls silly enough to tell his tale. And," Gillian smiled, "I count myself amongst those fools. However, it remains to be seen what toll I shall have to pay for it. But I digress.

Grimdire continued his reign of terror, capturing ship after ship and scuttling them once they were stripped of gold and goods. One can only imagine the trail of sunken vessels and hundreds of poor drowned sailors left in his wake.

But his hoard of treasure wasn't simply amassed out of greed, oh no, Grimdire had big plans. He saved every scrap of gold until he had enough wealth to commission a master shipbuilder to construct a fearsome galleon.

When it was launched, the shipbuilder had proudly named it The Golden Glory, but Grimdire made him change it to The

Rotten Blight, for he'd sworn he'd become the darkest blight ever to sail the seven seas.

The Blight was at sea for over a dozen years, robbing small fleets and sinking their enemies. But soon the navy tripled their efforts and fought back, harder than ever.

Finally, facing armadas that even The Rotten Blight couldn't down, Grimdire and his crew were driven to the ends of the earth and forced to hide wherever they could find cover.

They kept constant watch and only dared to raise their sails in the dead of night. And so it was by chance that they drifted, one moonless midnight, to an island yet to be named Whidbey and hid there in the sea mists as they bided their time.

Whidbey was a very different place back then. It was covered with ancient forests and inhabited by native tribes. There were other settlers too, though you won't find any records of them. But the one caught up in this terrible tale was named Ragnhild, a witch said to have been the descendant of a prominent Viking lord. How this despicable creature arrived at a place so far from her home is anyone's guess, although it was said she swooped down from the sky like a wretched, evil bird.

Soon Ragnhild was discovered to be living deep in the woods, and within no time the native tribes moved as far from her settlement as they could, for she was filled with the most terrible, violent darkness. But before they fled, they sought to disarm her of her weapon; a magical staff that seemed to hold the key to her power.

One night, their brave shaman snuck into her house. Silent as a shadow, he stole her staff and cast it into the sea; for he knew most witches had a terrible fear of the water. As the staff sank, he called a fearsome beast up from the murk to guard its resting place. And there it lay, safe and sound, until Captain Grimdire happened upon the island under a veil of darkness.

Evil attracts evil the same way bewildered mice will draw in snakes, so it wasn't long before Grimdire and Ragnhild crossed paths. But rather than destroying each other, which was exactly what they'd both secretly considered, they made a deal.

Grimdire agreed to recover Ragnhild's staff, and in return, she promised to use it to cast a spell, one that would grant Grimdire and his men eternal life and render The Rotten Blight unsinkable. That was their deal, forged at midnight in the dark depths of the forest.

The next morning, Ragnhild gave Grimdire the moon snail shell that she'd stolen from the tribe as they'd fled."

Gillian paused and took a sip of lemonade and her eyes wandered back to the windows like she was expecting someone.

"Why? What did the moon snail shell do?" Zach asked, barely hiding his impatience.

"I'm sorry," Gillian said, "I lost myself for a moment. The shell had been carved by the shaman and he played it like a whistle or flute. It was said to be a magical object and a means to summon the beast guarding the staff; a giant, fearsome octopus.

Now, Ragnhild had raised the creature herself once, but as soon as she'd seen it she knew it was too much even for her to wrestle with on her own. So she told Grimdire where the staff lay and he and his men loaded their cannons and set sail.

As they reached the spot, a terrible storm reared up along the horizon and the sea became a restless, treacherous thing. Undaunted, Grimdire raised the shell to his lips and blew into it, summoning the octopus from where it lurked.

The beast rose, tentacles writhing, each as thick and long as a tree trunk, and it stared at Grimdire with eyes so large they dwarfed the ship's wheel. And Grimdire stared back, his gaze as fearsome as the beast's. "Now!" he called.

At his command his men hurled a barrel of gunpowder over the gunwale and the octopus reached up and seized it. As its tentacles coiled and twisted in the air, Grimdire's best sharpshooter fired. *Boom!* The barrel exploded in a blaze of fire, right in the poor creatures' face, blinding it and causing it to writhe in torment.

The beast swam away, half ablaze, its moans and roars so great they echoed along the distant mountains. And in the chaos, Grimdire dove overboard into the dark, churning sea.

Down and down he swam until he reached the ocean floor, and there, in a wooden cage that he tore open with his bare hands, was the staff.

Prize in hand, he swam back up, boarded the Blight, and they sailed back to shore, victorious.

Soon Ragnhild emerged from her lair, her wicked eyes gleaming with triumph.

"Now, witch, make us eternal and the Blight unsinkable," Grimdire commanded.

At first, she was reluctant to waste even a lick of magic on them, but then she remembered how well armed they were. So she kept her word and granted them eternal life. She also enchanted the hull of the ship. Every board was rendered eternally sound and impenetrable, except one which laid nestled against the keel, in a place the captain would never look. This she did, because she didn't trust Grimdire, and her suspicions were soon proven right, for the moment her spells took hold he ordered his men to fire on her.

The night was long and loud and bright with the flash of rifle fire. Under such a barrage, any ordinary soul would have died ten times over. But Ragnhild was far from ordinary. By dawn however, even she couldn't heal her wounds, and knew she wasn't long for this world.

Grimdire stood over her, seized the staff, broke it over his knee and tossed it into her campfire, for he knew he couldn't wield it and didn't want anyone else to either.

Leaving Ragnhild to die, he and his men boarded The Rotten Blight, eager to test its new prowess upon the seas. They cheered, their hearts filled with vengeance and a wanton desire for destruction. "We'll scuttle and rob every worthy vessel upon the seven seas," Captain Grimdire announced, "until ours is the only one standing!"

Buoyed with dark excitement, and so consumed with triumphant anticipation for the future, they failed to look behind them.

Ragnhild peered down from the bluff, taking her final breaths. In her bloodied hands she cradled the charred remains of her staff. They lay in her palms, splintered and blackened, but still bearing power.

With a deep, heavy moan, Ragnhild summoned their magic, bolstering it with the last of the sorcery twisting through her vengeful heart. She focused it all into a hex; the darkest, most powerful she'd ever uttered.

"Curse you Captain Grimdire. Curse you and your wretched crew!"

She fell to her knees, her malevolent gaze fixed on the retreating ship as an eerie sea mist rose, one that would wrap itself around each and every man until they were as snug and tight as a spider's cocoon.

"You will lose your beloved ship before sunrise, and wander, half dead half damned until the ends of this world. For every moment of this cursed existence you'll long for your precious galleon as it lies in a lost lonely grave at the bottom of the sea."

And then she added a barbarous spin to her curse. That Grimdire and his crew would have leave to search for their galleon twice each century but only within the space of three days. And if they could find it and remain onboard until the dawn on the fifth of July, for the fourth was the very eve of her destruction, then they would live full lives once more.

But, as a final twist of the knife, she made them frail to the sun and light, making the search for their ship even harder. Finally, she used the last of the magic to bewitch the octopus and ordered it to hunt them forevermore.

With her curse laid, Ragnhild fell to the dirt, her vision dimming as tentacles broke from the waves below and the octopus began its terrible quest.

Soon, Grimdire realized there was treachery afoot. First, he and his men found themselves surrounded by a spectral mist that seemed to leak from their very pores. And then he heard the beast.

Grimdire turned, spyglass in hand, and found it pursuing them through the water.

Now, the octopus may have been blinded from its first encounter from Grimdire, but it was nimble enough to slip below the waves as they fired cannonball after cannonball upon it.

On and on they sailed along the island's lengthy shoreline, dogged by the heavy sea mist. And as The Rotten Blight came to a moaning halt, they screamed in terror. Something had seized the ship's hull and the sound of splintering, wrenching wood filled the air.

Grimdire raced below deck to find water flooding the ship's hold. The Rotten Blight was sinking fast, far too fast for them to recover the treasures they'd stowed there.

"Abandon ship!" Grimdire cried. He and his crew leaped overboard and swam for shore.

Finally, they reached land and trudged along the stony beach as the last of The Rotten Blight sank below the waves.

"Curse this island!" Captain Grimdire howled. He glanced around, searching for someone to take his ire out on, but the rising sun scorched his eyes and he was forced to retreat.

Soon, they fled to the shadows of the trees and set up camp while they waited for night to fall so they could recover their gold. But as the fog stole over them, it befuddled their minds and sent them wandering. In no time they were quite lost and unable to remember where The Rotten Blight had sunk.

Eventually, driven half mad by time and the relentless fog, they stumbled upon a moored ship. After a fearsome battle with the crew they heisted the vessel and set sail. But no matter how far they traveled, the mists plagued them.

Then, on the second of July, after fifty fruitless years of searching for The Rotten Blight, a putrefied, half dead gull landed on the deck of the purloined ship. It carried a parchment, and the message scrawled upon it was short and simple. Ragnhild had left a legacy of sorts; three magical treasure chests. The first one contained a map and a clue to where the second chest could be discovered. And the second chest held a clue to where the third chest lay buried. And that third chest held the moon snail shell and a map marking the exact spot where The Rotten Blight sank. In other words, everything they'd need to recover their ship.

"Where are the chests?" Grimdire demanded, but the bird had no answers and with a swipe of his hand it toppled from the rail and plunged to the bottom of the sea." Gillian paused and studied each of us in turn. "And that's the legend of Captain Grimdire, and now I've told it to you."

"That's the best thing I've ever heard! Much better than I remember!" Zach shook his head in wonder. "But how comes no one else knows about it?"

"Because the Society of the Owl and Wolf wanted it that way," Gillian said. "The original members of the Society found the first chest a hundred years ago, quite by accident. Or maybe it wasn't accident, who knows? It appeared to them just as the three days were elapsing and they pulled the map for the location of the second chest from inside. But they couldn't dig up the second chest, not for fifty years, and when the time was right it was their sons and daughters who went searching for it. But as they reached it, they heard the tolling of a ship's bell and a terrible fog swept in from nowhere, so they abandoned their quest, terrified at the prospect of Grimdire slaughtering them and finding the final chest."

"And now fifty years have passed once more and they're still too scared to dig up the chests," Jacob said.

"Scared for all the right reasons," Gillian replied. "Because now it's not just Grimdire searching, it's those strangers as well. And there's every possibility one or the other might finally dig them up this time."

"Which means we need get to them first," Zach said. "That way we can hide the moon shell and map where no one will ever find them."

Gillian looked at each of us with a slow, earnest look. "I can't stop you from trying, and I'm sure you'll do a better job of stopping Grimdire than the Society has so far."

"Is this why you're leaving?" Emily asked.

"Mostly," Gillian said. "I believe it's only a matter of time before Grimdire finds the chests. But maybe you'll find them first and spoil his chances. Either way, I'm not willing to risk it."

"We'll get them first," Jacob vowed. "It's not like we have any choice."

"Correct," Gillian said, "Because if Grimdire finds The Rotten Blight I have no doubt he'll take the most horrific revenge." She clutched her plastic cup and stared at the melting ice cubes, before adding, "I'm sorry I can't help you, I-"

She stopped as a branch snapped outside, and as she snuck to the window, her eyes were wild with pure, utter terror.

16

WHAT IS BURIED

"**I**s someone out there?" I asked, my voice cracking with my rising fear.

Gillian glanced around the trees, and slowly, some of the fear left her eyes. She shook her head. "I don't see anybody. Not that that counts for anything these days. Wait here." She vanished from the room.

I joined the others at the window. The woods looked still and empty, but as she'd said, that didn't necessarily mean they were. I scanned the branches, searching for the creepy old parrot. If it was there, it was well hidden.

"Here," Gillian said, returning with a book. It was her collection of myths and legends. She handed it to Zach. "This is for you. All of you. It's exactly the same as the one you've been checking out at the library, but this one has the legend of Captain Grimdire intact. Keep it safe, this is the last copy I have."

"Don't you want to keep it?" Emily asked.

"Yeah, I could just scan the missing pages, that way we'd have a copy," Jacob said, as he glanced through the apps on his phone and opened one.

"No," Gillian said, "I want you to have this. If you're going to see this through, then you're going to need a hard copy that can't be accidentally, or should I say deliberately deleted. And who knows," she gave us a wistful smile, "you may need to refer to it again in future if you survive this challenge. Now, may I see the map?"

I pulled it from my pocket and unfurled it carefully. Gillian took a magnifying glass from a crate and swept it across the crumpled paper. "Ah, yes. That looks familiar."

"We think it's Double Bluff beach," Emily said.

"Yes, there's Mount Rainier, so that has to be the view from Double Bluff." She flipped it over and read, *"Find a hard old heart half buried in the sand, five steps south dig with your hand.* Whatever does that mean?" she asked, as she handed me back the map.

"No idea," Zach said, "do you want to help us find out?"

Gillian shook her head. "I wish I could. But," she cast another furtive glance to the window, "my time here is done. Now, let me see you out." She walked us to the door and opened it just wide enough so we could squeeze through. "Be careful... I... I'm sorry you're facing this on your own, but it is what it is. Perhaps you'll pick up where the Society of the Owl and Wolf left off."

"Good luck with your move," I said, knowing exactly how much fun that was.

"Thank you, Dylan. Now, take care." Gillian closed the door.

"What now?" I asked.

"Now we go and dig the chest up. Finally!" Zach grinned, but I saw the glint of uneasiness in his eyes and I felt the same. Excitement at the possibility of finding treasure and fear of whatever else might be buried there with it.

"We're going to need shovels," Jacob said to Zach. "What have we got left in club funds?"

Zach rifled through a worn old wallet that looked like it was probably a hand-me-down from his father. "Three dollars and forty-seven cents."

"That might be enough if we can find one at the thrift store," Emily suggested.

"It's still not going to be enough," Jacob said.

I took a deep breath. As my grandma used to say, in for a penny, in for a pound. "I've got some money," I said. I still had the cash Mr. Ovalhide had given me.

"Great, let's go and find our treasure," Zach said as he sped off through the woods.

We raced back to town and bought two shovels that were on offer, and a compass which Jacob thought we might need seeing as the one hidden inside the hollowed book was broken.

Then we stopped at the grocery store and I bought ice-cream for everyone because it was hot, and I was feeling glad that I'd met my new friends, even Zach. They were helping me, they were putting themselves in danger and ultimately that was down to me. But I didn't say that of course. Instead, I smiled and joined in the discussion of how we'd spend our riches once we found them.

AN HOUR LATER, WE GOT OFF THE BUS AND CYCLED DOWN what felt like an endless road leading to the beach, our wheels whirring, and the sea breeze cool against the heat.

Double Bluff was a long, curved beach bounded by a high sandy bluff pitted with rocks. The trees that topped it were thin, crooked things and at the bottom tangled piles of driftwood marked the tide line. In places, we saw forts and structures that people had made from the pale salty wood. We trudged past them through the sand and as we neared the water, scuttling hermit crabs and tiny sea urchins shifted in their tide pools. People smiled and said hello as we walked by and called to their dogs as they raced toward the calm lapping waves.

We made sure no one was watching as we checked the map again and set off toward the rocks.

The tide was out and I could see Seattle in the distance. It looked so small, like a toy city, with Mount Rainier hulking behind it, giant and ghostly in the smog.

Ahead, just past a curve in the beach, was a huge rock embedded in the sand. It was covered with barnacles, limpets and strands of seaweed, and from where we stood even I could see it looked vaguely heart-shaped.

"That's got to be it!" Emily said, "the hard old heart!"

I glanced around again. There were still a lot of people around, but thankfully there was no sign of the strangers or Grimdire's cursed sea mist.

"Find a hard old heart half buried in the sand," Jacob said, reading the clue on the back again, "and five steps south dig with your hand."

"What about shovels?" Zach asked, "I mean Dylan's just paid for them," he said, holding one over his head. "The least we can do is use them."

"Whoever wrote that clue probably didn't have a shovel, Zach," Emily said, "I think it's safe to say we can use whatever we need."

Jacob held the compass steady as he walked around the rock. "This is south," he said, holding up his finger, before taking five steps. "The X should be here." He made a line in the sand with the heel of his sneaker. "Except we don't know how tall the person that made the map was, so it could be anywhere around this point."

We began digging, sludging spadefuls of heavy wet sand onto the beach. I paused as a big, adult-sized shadow fell over me. I spun around, expecting to find the strangers behind me or worse, Captain Grimdire.

It was an old man with a scratchy beard and quick, inquisitive eyes. "And what pray tell are you digging for, young people?" he asked.

"I..." I didn't know what to say.

"We're making a sand castle. Is that okay?" Zach answered, looking the man up and down in his usual dismissive way.

"You don't have a bucket. You need a bucket to make a decent sand castle," the old man replied. It seemed he was warming to Zach's challenge.

"True," Zach said, "but I have buckets of imagination, believe me."

The old man gazed at him for a moment, and then the rest of us. "Looks to me like all you're *making* is an unsightly mess. But to each his own, I suppose." He gave a considerable sigh before finally wandering away, moaning and muttering as he went.

I watched him for a moment, and then, before I could get back to digging, I heard a heavy, solid *thunk!*

Emily gazed into the hole at her feet. Her eyes were wide as a slow, cautious smile lit her face. She glanced around to make sure we were alone. We were. "Found it!" she whispered.

We sank to our knees and dug around the ancient-looking chest. It was smaller than I'd imagined and the wood was worn, pitted, full of cracks and heavily discolored with age. Emily and I lifted it out and set it down on the sand. We gazed at it, but no one made a move to unfasten the brass latch sealing it shut.

"Aren't you going to open it?" Zach asked, impatiently.

"You should do the honors," Emily offered.

"I'm not the one who dug it up."

"But you would have," I said, "if Emily hadn't found it first."

"I think *you* should open it, Dylan," Zach said, "you're the newest member. It can be your initiation ceremony. Right, Jacob?"

"I don't know?" Jacob said. "We've never had an initiation ceremony before. We don't even have a name for our... club... or whatever it is."

"Then maybe it should be you, Jacob," Zach said.

Jacob sighed. "We just found buried treasure, and we're all too freaked out to open it?" He shook his head and reached into his pocket. "Why don't we toss a coin? Whoever loses the toss first opens the chest. Right?"

We nodded slowly like we were being led to our certain deaths. Jacob held his hand out. "I'm calling heads. You?" he asked.

Zach and Emily both said heads while I called tails. And then I wished I hadn't, but before I could change my call the coin was flipping in a gleaming silver arc.

"Heads," Jacob said, barely hiding his relief.

"It's you then," Zach clapped his hand on my shoulder. "Good luck." He turned to the others. "We should probably back up. Give him some space."

"You think it's going to explode, don't you," I said.

"The thought might have crossed my mind," Zach admitted as he stepped away. Emily and Jacob gave me deeply sympathetic looks as they joined him.

My fingers trembled as I reached for the latch.

Closing my eyes, I cracked the lid, my heart racing as a terrible, angry hiss came from inside.

17

THE RIDDLE

My fingers trembled and I almost dropped the lid as the hissing grew louder. Slowly, I opened my eyes. Thick green smoke spilled from the box, obscuring its contents. Then the smoke began to glow as it curled through the air, forming a shape. A skull.

I felt its sightless eyes staring into mine, assessing me like an angry teacher might. It was as if the skull could see it all; my thoughts, my fears, everything inside me. I froze. The beach and sky blurred away and all I saw were those hollow eyes.

The skull's mouth opened as it hissed a single word. *"Yessssss."*

Yes, what? Yes, I was cursed? Yes, my heart was about to burst? It certainly felt like it.

The empty eyes grew wider and then it grinned as it began to fade. Suddenly I realized the others were watching and I could feel the warm sun on my arms again and hear the gentle lap of the tide.

Hissssss.

The form of the skull broke apart. Then the smoke thinned and wafted away.

"Wow!" Zach said, "you're braver than I thought. I'd have chucked that box straight into the water and been halfway up the bluff by now."

I wasn't brave, I'd been frozen with terror, but there didn't seem to be any point making a big announcement about it.

"What's inside?" Jacob asked as he and Emily joined me.

The chest was lined with ragged old velvet and there, in the middle, was a corked bottle containing a scroll of paper bound by frayed red ribbon. Slowly, carefully, Emily unrolled it and began to read.

"If you're reading these words you passed the test, had you not, you'd be stricken with a most final rest. Now seek the shell on a spot of tiny land, where the geoduck clams thrive and the herons stand. Nine paces north from the wind bent tree, you'll find a map to a forbidden secret hidden beneath the sea."

"What does that mean?" I asked.

Jacob fixed his glasses in place as he paced and repeated the riddle. "Tiny land," he said, over and over.

"Tiny land," Zach repeated over and over with his finger on his chin, as if he were a statue of some old philosopher. Now and then he peered at Jacob as Emily read and re-read the note.

While they puzzled it out I refilled the holes we'd dug and examined the chest. I wondered exactly who had buried it, and when. Had it been the witch or one of her enchanted underlings? I set the chest down, hoping it wasn't contagious. Could you catch evil? It was starting to feel like anything was possible.

"Baby Island!" Jacob shouted. He slapped Zach on the shoulder even though he'd done nothing to help.

"Yes, *on a spot of tiny land*, that has to be it!" Emily said.

"It was right on the tip of my tongue," Zach said but I was pretty sure that wasn't true.

"What's Baby Island?" I asked. Jacob pulled out his cell phone, opened his map app, and showed me a tiny scrap of land just off the shore off Whidbey Island. I'd never heard of it, but that wasn't exactly surprising. "Have you been there before?" I asked.

"Not really. We've cruised by it in my parent's boat a few times, but we've never stopped," Jacob said. "There really isn't much to it, but we've seen people out there once or twice. You can walk right over to it when the tide's low."

"We should get going," Zach said. "If we hurry, we can catch the three o' clock bus."

"No, it's miles away," Jacob said, "even if we get the bus, it'll take too long and I need to be home by five."

Emily held her phone out. "Fair enough. Anyway, the tide's coming in. And there's no way I'm swimming to the island."

"Me neither," Zach said, "especially when there's a monstrous octopus prowling around."

"Yeah, it's too risky," Jacob said, "we should wait for low tide."

I was relieved. Digging up the box had been amazing, but I felt like I'd hit my adventure quota for the day. "Does anyone want the chest?" I asked. A part of me wanted to take it home, a larger part of me didn't.

"Yeah! I'll take it," Emily said, "if no one else wants it." She placed it carefully into her backpack. With that, there was no longer any visible evidence that anything extraordinary had just happened. People walked by, frisbees whizzed through the air and dogs rolled around in the seaweed. It was like there were two different worlds; theirs, and ours.

We caught the next bus heading toward home, got off at

the closest stop and cycled the rest of the way. The sun filtered through the trees and the breeze was cool. Soon we were back in Langley, where we went our own ways and promised to meet early the next day.

"You look pleased," Mom said as I got home. "Did you have a nice day with your friends?"

"Yep," I said. And we found a buried map hidden by a witch who cursed a pirate. But I can't tell you that, I thought. It was our secret and ours alone.

"You've already made friends here?" Jamie asked. "They must be idiots." He rolled his eyes, but I caught an odd tone in his voice, like he was jealous or feeling left out. I almost felt sorry for him. With his personality, it'd take him ages to make friends on the island, and when he did, they'd be horrible. Some things in life were certain.

My eyes stung and watered as I helped Dad chop us some onions for dinner. Of course, Jamie said I was crying, but the truth was I hadn't felt so happy in a long time.

❧

I COULDN'T STOP THINKING ABOUT EVERYTHING THAT HAD happened and before I knew it, it was time for bed. I got into my pj's and drifted right off. And when I woke during the night, I was smiling from my dreams.

But that didn't last long.

I'd forgotten to draw my curtains and dark shadows from the branches outside stretched across the wall. Among them was the ghostly shape of a parrot, squat and stumpy with a long curved beak.

Its shadowy head swiveled, and I heard a low rasping call.

I sat up, rigid, but when I looked again, the bird had gone.

❧ 18 ❧

NIGHTINGALE LANE

I called Zach and Emily as soon as I got up that morning. Zach sounded seriously depressed, like he'd just been told he'd caught some terrible disease. "We're going to the other side," he said.

"What?" I thought of old horror movies where people sat in dark circles tracing fingers across Ouija boards as smoky ghosts lurked in the gloom behind them.

"You know, taking the ferry over, going off the island. Our mom wants to go shopping," Emily said, her voice quieter as she spoke on their other phone. "Call Jacob. Maybe you guys can go check out Baby Island while we're gone."

"Or," Zach added, "they could wait for us to get back. I checked, there's a low tide tonight just after seven. We could get Violet to take us there."

"I don't think we should tell anyone else about this," I said. Especially not their sister.

"We're not going to tell her a thing," Zach said, "she'll just drive us to the beach, then she'll wander off to meet her stupid boyfriend. She won't care what we're doing. Trust me."

"You really think she'll take us?" I asked.

"Yep," Emily said, "we've got dirt on her."

"*Serious* dirt," Zach added. "Right now we could make her do almost anything we want. It's like owning a robot. Or a zombie. Or a robot zombie. It's pretty neat."

"Nice," I said, wondering how I could get serious dirt on Jamie too.

"Call Jacob and tell him to be at our place by six thirty. We'll definitely be back by then," Zach said. "Mom's got yoga tonight, and she never misses it so we'll be on that five o'clock ferry come what may."

"Okay, I'll see you later, I guess," I said. I shivered as I thought of the ferry and crossed my fingers that they'd make it back safely without any run-ins with the octopus or Captain Grimdire. They were both out there. Somewhere.

❧

I SPENT THE REST OF THE DAY HELPING MOM AND DAD unpack boxes until we finally crushed the last one and stamped on it for good luck. The stamping was mom's idea and while I wasn't sure it would actually bring us luck, I felt like we could use all the help we could get.

It was strange doing chores and playing happy families knowing there were two maniacs and a cursed pirate crew on the trail of a sunken galleon out there. And that we were the ones holding the clue to finding it.

Before I knew it, it was late afternoon. I cycled over to meet my friends, wondering what we'd find this time. Another smoke skull? Or maybe something worse...

I dropped my bike on the lawn outside Zach and Emily's house.

"Hey Dylan!"

There was a *shhh* of brakes as Jacob skidded up behind me with such force his backpack jerked to the side then thudded into him. "How's it going, Jacob?" I asked.

He looked flustered like he'd been cycling really fast. "Not good! I just saw the strangers... you know... the ones you were hiding from that day at the library. I think I know where they live!"

"Where?"

"In the woods off Nightingale Lane. They just stopped on the side of the road, got out of their battered old car and strode off into the trees."

"Do you think they were digging for treasure there?"

"No, they had bags of groceries, it looked like they were going home."

"I guess the woods is a good place to live if you're hiding out," I said, "plenty of shadows."

"Exactly!"

We turned as the front door opened and Zach appeared. "Afternoon, gents," he said, with a fake British accent. He saluted us, messing up his already messed up hair. "I packed supplies," he said, pointing to his backpack. It was the exact same olive-green as Jacob's.

"We're only going to be there for an hour, right?" Jacob asked.

"Yes," Zach agreed, "but you never know what could happen. I've got fruit, drinks and a few candy bars. Just in case."

And then Jacob told him about the strangers.

"Jeez, now I wish Nightingale Lane was further away," Zach said, glancing up the street, "like a few thousand miles. Preferably on the side of an active volcano...or a sinkhole. They're probably cooped up in that old shack. No one's lived there for years."

"That place is creep central," Jacob said, "imagine the spiders and-" He stopped as Violet shoved the front door open. Her jaw moved fast as she stormed across the yard chewing her gum. Somehow she looked even more irritated than the first time I'd seen her. She unlocked the dusty, dirt-streaked car door and climbed in, her head colliding with a pair of furry dice hanging from the mirror. "Ready?" she called. But it wasn't really a question.

Then Emily appeared. "Hi," she called to me and Jacob. I was about to reply when a thin bird-shaped shadow glided across the sidewalk. I looked up but there was nothing there.

"Is he coming, or what?" Violet asked.

She was talking about me. I shrugged, climbed into the back of the car and sat beside Emily.

"One hour. Right?" Violet said as she peeled out, stirring up a dusty cloud.

"That's what we agreed," Zach said.

"We didn't agree anything. You blackmailed me you little-"

"No, no, no. It's not blackmail," Zach cut in, "it's a trade. I have incriminating information, you have a car. You're swapping your driving skills for my silence. You're getting a bargain and you know it."

Violet muttered something that sounded like every bad word I'd ever heard as she headed out of town on a long wooded road. Finally, after we'd driven for what felt like forever, she slowed at a sharp bend and turned onto a short street lined with houses. "One hour," she said, "and don't test me, I'm not going to wait around, that beach smells like dog breath."

The car jerked to a stop and we climbed out.

"She's right," Zach said as he took a deep sniff, "it does smell like dog breath."

"Mixed with rotten fish," Emily added.

"And week old vomit," Jacob finished.

We made our way down toward the shoreline. In the distance, across a muddy strip of wet land, was a tiny island with a single tree. The tide was out, and the sea was calm as we walked along the mud flat, shovels in hand, the ground crunching and popping below our sneakers.

"It sounds like we're walking on a carpet of bubble wrap," Zach said, "which funnily enough, is something I've always wanted to try."

"It's good to have ambitions," Emily said, rolling her eyes.

"It sounds more like popcorn," Jacob said.

"That'd be even better," Zach said. "A carpet made of popcorn..."

I was barely listening as I gazed ahead. The sun had vanished behind the low grey clouds sailing across the sky. It seemed the June gloom had extended into July. I glanced back, worried we might be being followed but no one was around. It was like we had the whole beach to ourselves, but then I caught an odd glint of light near the houses in the distance. What was it?

"Hey, hurry up!" Zach called.

I hadn't realized they'd gotten so far ahead of me. I ran to catch up.

We reached the island and Jacob paused by the tree. He pulled the compass from his pocket, turned a few times, and pointed ahead. "That way!" He took nine steps and thrust his shovel into the ground. I half expected to hear another *thunk*, but there was just a dull swish of sand as he began to dig.

Soon, the area around us was full of holes. I shivered as the wind blew. It felt like it had suddenly gotten a lot colder.

Crunch.

"Here!" Zach cried. Inside the hole at his feet was the corner of a wooden lid, just like the chest from the day before.

We dropped to our knees, reached inside the hole and lifted the box out.

"Who's going to open it?" Zach asked. There was a troubled look in his eyes.

"You found it," I said.

"So I get to decide who opens it. Finders rights," Zach said.

"That's not a thing," Emily said.

"Nope. Never heard of it," Jacob added.

"Me neither," I said.

"Fine. We'll toss a coin then," Zach said. "Go on Jacob, you're the coin master."

"Since when did I take on that responsibility?" Jacob asked, raising an eyebrow over his glasses.

"Since yesterday," Zach said. "You did a great job. It was probably the best coin tossing I've ever seen, actually. Now, flip it!"

"Right." Jacob pulled out his wallet.

We called our bets and this time Zach lost. "Great," he said. Then his face fell and he stared at the chest like it was a loaded gun aimed at his heart. "Right. Well." He reached for it but pulled his hands away. "How should I..."

"Oh, just get out the way!" Emily pushed past him, but I saw her cross her fingers before she opened the catch.

Whoooossssshhhh

Bright purple smoke snaked up from the chest. Slowly it gathered like it had a mind of its own, and then it formed another skull, its hollow eyes staring at Emily. A moment later it turned in the air and regarded each of us. *"Yessssss."* It hissed, before breaking apart and drifting away on the rising breeze.

Inside was another bottle with a rolled scroll of parchment, and the large pearly white shell of a moon snail. It shone, almost as if someone had polished it and as I looked closer I saw it was pierced along the spiral like the holes of a flute.

There was also a pattern carved into its surface; an enormous octopus, its tentacles writhing, its lantern-like eyes almost glowing in the chest's gloom.

"Amazing," Zach said. He pulled the shell out and raised it to his lips. "Ready?" He gave us a mischievous grin.

"No!" Jacob and I cried at the same time. Thankfully Emily snatched it from him.

"You don't want to see that octopus," I said. "Believe me! Especially not when we're stuck out here in the middle of nowhere on our own. "

"We're going to have to deal with it at some point," Jacob said.

"No, we don't," Emily shook her head, "not if we hide the shell and map until the fifth of July. After that Grimdire can't do anything, and neither can the strangers."

"Not for another fifty years," Jacob added, "and humans will probably be living in space by then."

"I won't," Zach said. "I'll be king of the robot overlords and the true master of Earth."

"Of course you will," Emily said.

"Maybe we should just destroy the map and shell," I said. "If we do that, Grimdire wouldn't be able to find his ship."

"They're enchanted, remember? I'm no expert," Zach said, "but I'm pretty sure that means they can't be destroyed because if it were that easy, someone would have done it already."

"Right." I guessed it made about as much sense as everything else on this crazy goose chase.

"So like Emily said, we should hide them," Jacob said.

"Good plan." Zach picked up the chest, opened the bottle and peered at the scroll. "But maybe we should read the clue first. Try and figure out exactly where the galleon is. It can't hurt, can it?"

"Okay." Emily took it from him, untied the ribbon, and carefully opened it. On one side of the paper was a map and on the other a message. Emily read it slowly. *"If you've come this far, then you've survived the skull. Had you not your lives would be null. Blow the shell and raise the beast, so Captain Grimdire becomes its final feast. You'll find the Blight in the depths of the cove, where the seagulls hunt and the mussels rove."*

"What does that mean?" I asked.

Jacob pulled out his phone and snapped a picture of the parchment. "I'm going to need to put my thinking cap on and think this through."

"Well then I'm going to need to put on my thinking hat," Zach said. "Watch out, it's six feet tall and needs a team of monkeys to keep it upright."

"You're an idiot," Emily said.

"I know you are, but what am I?" Zach asked, and then he cried out as she punched him in the arm.

I laughed, glad for the humor but Jacob ignored us as he gazed into his phone, contemplating the picture he'd taken of the clue. Zach examined the map again and passed me it so I could take a closer look. I had no idea what the clue meant, but the parchment was really neat in a crumpled, timeworn way.

"Penn Cove!" Jacob said. "There's a mussel farm there!"

"That's exactly what I was about to say," Zach said.

"Of course you were." Emily rolled her eyes. "Come on then, we should head back."

We were about to start back across the island, when we froze.

Crunch. Crunch. Crunch.

It was coming from the strip of land that linked the two islands, and the noise was getting louder.

I turned to find wisps of fog swirling through the air. I

couldn't see anything but grey. It was like Whidbey Island had vanished.

Crunch. Crunch. Crunch.

Footsteps! They were charging across the shell-strewn flat, coming right toward us.

It sounded like there were dozens of them.

CRUNCH TIME

*C*runch. *Crunch. Crunch.*

Whoever was there had almost reached the island.

"Where'd all this fog come from?" Zach's hand trembled as he swept at the mist.

Oh..." My words froze as a tall, heavy silhouette appeared. I could just make out the crumpled hat, and a long gleaming beard.

It was the man I'd seen on the ship.

Captain Grimdire.

He was huge; even taller than my dad. As he stepped forward the mist seemed to move with him, like a giant rag-grey cloak. It thinned in places, revealing further details.

His battered hat hung low over his face, but I could see his bright blue eyes. They were bloodshot around the edges. His long crooked nose jutted out and his lips were thin and cruel.

Grimdire gave a triumphant grin, revealing a golden tooth that gleamed through the mist.

A terrible new stench wafted through the air. It smelled of

mold, dead things and sunless places. "Come here," he said in a thick, rasping old English accent.

Shadowy figures shifted in the fog as his crew slowly surrounded us.

"No," I said.

Zach stood beside me, Jacob and Emily were a few feet away. Between them and us was another pirate. It was the one that had come to my house in the dead of night, and perched on his shoulder was the tattered, putrid parrot. It studied us with its beady eyes.

"You..." I said dumbly.

A smile curled across his face and one of his teeth fell out. "Arrrr," he growled.

"Come," Grimdire said, "give us the shell and map, laddie boy." He held out a huge hand covered in a wormy old glove.

"What are we going to do?" Zach's voice was high and shrill.

"I..." I was petrified with terror.

"They've blocked the flats but we could swim for it," Emily called.

She had a point. If we ran for the tip of the island, we could swim back to shore. The water wasn't deep... was it? "I... I can't." My terror kicked in and I was sure that something would drag me down until I was as cold, rotten and dead as the pirates before us. I shuddered.

"Enough," Captain Grimdire shouted as he slipped an ancient cutlass from the sheath by his side. "Either hand over the map and shell, or I'll take them, along with your pretty little heads. What's it to be?"

"Wait!" Jacob threw his backpack down and rooted through it, his face stern with concentration. He pulled out his bike lamp. "Remember the legend!" He switched the light on and aimed it at the nearest pirate.

The beam shone through the mist, striking the pirate's chest. A glowing hole of light burned through his filthy old shirt. "Yarr!" he yelled and blundered away, throwing up a smoking hand against the light.

I didn't have a flashlight but Zach did. He fumbled as he pulled it from his backpack and jammed his thumb down on the button. "Have some of this!" he shouted, wide eyed, as he scorched a glowing hole in the pirate before him. The pirates hissed and drew away.

The tables had turned.

At least that's what I thought until suddenly, Emily started screaming.

✦ 20 ✦

HOCUS POCUS

Emily tried to wrench herself free from the old pirate who had seized her by the scruff of her neck. He grinned as he tightened his grip. Her face grew pale and her eyes began to roll.

It was like he was draining her life away.

"Emily!" I shouted.

"No!" Zach's flashlight sliced through the fog. The pirate hissed and drew back, dragging Emily with him. Then he opened his mouth, blowing out a stream of mist that formed a curtain around them, blocking Zach's light.

I could just make out her panicked eyes as she seemed to stir awake.

"Take it!" Zach threw the flashlight. She caught it and aimed it behind her. The pirate gave a tortured cry and let her go.

I glanced back as Grimdire shambled toward us. "I'm tired of this folly," he said. "Give me the map and the shell or I'll take yer lives. Right here and now."

Emily and Jacob were free, but a mob of pirates stood between us and them, and more were closing in.

"Get help!" I cried to them, but the dense fog seemed to deaden my plea.

Jacob swung his flashlight toward the pirates. Some withdrew, but there were too many of them. "Take it!" He threw the light. It sailed over the pirate's heads. I caught it one handed as Jacob and Emily ran, vanishing into the mist, her beam of light swinging madly until it was swallowed up.

"I warned you, boy," Grimdire was almost on us.

I swung around, aiming the flashlight at his chest. "Die again, you-"

Nothing happened.

He didn't flinch. He didn't move a cursed muscle.

His smirk grew wider, his dry peeling lips clinging to his black stumpy teeth. The gold tooth flashed as he opened his coat. Below it was a plate of armor that looked like it had been made from old crab shells.

"I came prepared," Grimdire said. He waved a finger at me. "Your hocus-pocus won't work on me, laddie. By the day after tomorrow we'll be as real as rain. And when the Blight rises we will destroy this accursed island and everything on it. But I might spare you, if you hand over the shell and map. Now!" Evil shone in his glowing stare. It was all there, his delight in cruelty, and the countless lives he'd taken. I'd never looked into such horrible wicked eyes.

"No," I said, pretending I wasn't scared of him or the terrifying sword in his hand.

"No?" Grimdire cried. "No? Do you know what happens to men who say no to me?"

I shook my head. "I'm not a-"

"They become a feast for the fishes. Do you have any idea what it's like to drown, boy? To have your body picked apart by crabs, one scrap of flesh at a time. To have your bones shine nice and white on the bottom of the sea?"

I suddenly realized he'd been distracting me, that while I'd been listening to his terrible speech he'd somehow sidled up right beside Zach. It had happened so fast neither of us had noticed what he was up to.

Grimdire's hand shot out to seize Zach by his hair, but he missed as Zach shrieked and stumbled away.

"Here!" I threw the flashlight. "Run!" At least he could get away.

Zach didn't need telling twice. He stumbled off, wielding the flashlight as two pirates tried to close in on him. They roared with rage and staggered away with glowing holes gleaming in their ragged clothes.

It seemed like Zach was going to make it. By his laugh and the way he shouted, "Yes!" it seemed he thought so too. And then he tripped and fell. The flashlight bounced from his hand and vanished into the mist. A moment later I heard a loud splash.

Zach glanced up as Grimdire and his pirates bore down on him. There was a small break in the mist before me... it was my chance to escape.

My legs tensed. I prepared to run harder than I'd ever run before.

But I faltered. I couldn't leave Zach.

Instead of racing away, I sprinted past Grimdire, grabbed Zach with one hand and clenched the map in my other as I pulled him to his feet.

We were set to run when a black shape flew through the mist. I threw my hands up to guard my face and something snatched the map from my grip. I caught a glimpse of the parrot wheeling through the fog, the map grasped in its claws.

"We have the map!" Grimdire cried, raising his cutlass as he strode toward us. "Now give me the shell, boy!"

He swung the cutlass. I ducked. It sliced the air above my

head, bringing an aching cold draft. I sidestepped and tumbled back.

Grimdire was almost on me when something bounced off his face.

An orange?

I glanced back to find Zach rooting through his backpack. "Here! Try this one. An apple a day keeps the doctor away!"

The apple soared at Grimdire. He sliced it in two with his cutlass and as it hit the ground it turned from fresh and crisp to rotten brown and teeming with maggots.

If that was what his cutlass did to an apple, what would it do to us?

"You'll pay for that, laddie boy. You'll both pay!" The mist thickened around Grimdire and his body appeared more substantial. It was like he was becoming more real.

Zach reached into his bag and threw a banana. It sailed through the air and hit Grimdire's face with a solid thud. He stumbled away.

"Run!" I cried, ducking past Grimdire and seizing Zach's sleeve. We plunged through the mist, dodging pirates as we went.

The fog was like a never-ending wall of grey. Shadowy forms staggered toward us and I suddenly realized we'd lost our flashlight. Worse, I had no idea where we were going.

My panic grew but having Zach to look out for somehow made me feel stronger.

Thud. Thud. Thud.

Grimdire stomped after us. I could hear his ragged breath, hear his curses, and as I glanced back I saw dozens of dark forms closing in on us.

21

HEADS IT IS!

"**D**uck!" I shouted.

We dropped low as Grimdire's cutlass soared over our heads, slicing the mist, which was getting... lighter!

"We're almost there!" I cried, "Hurry!" I pulled Zach along. We plunged through the lifting fog and stumbled across the spit of land into daylight. The clouds broke and a ray of sunshine hit the beach, turning the sand from dusty grey to sparkling gold.

I glanced back to see Grimdire pacing along the gloomy shore of the little island. His pirates stood by him, a line of creepy dark figures lurking in the grey haze. They lifted their cutlasses and shouted with ragged rage, but stayed put, trapped by the beam of sunlight.

Jacob and Emily were waiting on the beach. They waved for us to hurry like we needed to be told. We ran until we reached them. Then we leaned over, resting our hands on our knees as we tried to catch our breaths.

"We're safe here," Emily said, "the sunlight's holding them back!"

I nodded. Baby Island was covered in mist but as it thinned, I caught sight of the dark silhouette of their ship. The tide was still low so we were well out of reach. Slowly the fog rolled away and a bell tolled as the pirates drifted back out to sea.

"What happened?" Jacob asked.

"I..." I shook my head. "I lost the map."

"And saved my life!" Zach said. He told the others what had happened, and he didn't need to exaggerate because the story was already wild enough.

It was still hard to believe it had happened. I'd never felt so proud in my life and my face reddened as Emily and Jacob grinned at me. Jamie was wrong; I *was* brave. Or at least I was when it counted. And if I could do it once, I could do it again...

"Also," Jacob said as Zach paused to catch his breath, "we didn't totally lose the map." He held his phone up. "I took a picture, remember?" He showed me the screen and there it was; the map of the cove I'd seen the other day, and right in its center a faded red-brown x.

"And, we've still got the shell," Emily added.

"What are we going to do with it?" I asked.

"We're going to use it." Emily said. "We're going to summon the octopus and end this once and for all."

I didn't like the idea, not one little bit. But I forced myself to be decisive and stood taller, which seemed to help. "Unless we find someone else to do it for us."

"There isn't anyone else," Jacob said. "No one's going to believe us. I know exactly what my parents would do if I told them what's been going on, they'd send me to the nut house."

"Mine too," Zach said distractedly.

"They've already got a room reserved there for you, Zach,"

Emily said. "But Jacob's right, this is up to us. We need to figure out what to do with this shell, until it's time to use it."

"What do you mean?" I asked.

"Well," she said, "we need to keep it safe. Obviously Grimdire's looking for it and that was a close call; it was totally within his grasp. We got lucky, but luck can go both ways; good and bad."

"We should hide it," Jacob whispered. He glanced around to make sure the coast was literally clear. "In a place no one will ever find it."

"Like where?" Zach asked.

Jacob positioned his glasses over the bridge of his nose and gazed at the sand. His face was blank. "I don't know."

"I don't think we should risk leaving it anyplace where we can't keep an eye on it," I said.

"Yeah, one of us needs to guard it." Zach looked at each of us in turn. "Who's going to do that?"

"Well," Jacob said, "the pirates don't seem to know where *you* live," he said glancing at Zach.

Zach shook his head as his gaze fell on me. "Dylan should take it. He's the bravest."

I was about to disagree when I faltered. "Alright," I said, before I could stop myself. "I'll take it. I'll stay up and make sure no one steals it in the night. I can do that, I've stayed up all night before." It was true, I had, but only because I'd thought there was a ghost in my old room, which had turned out to be just another of Jamie's twisted pranks.

"I don't know..." Jacob said.

"Me neither," Emily added, "the pirates know where you live."

"Then it's two against two," Zach said. "We need to flip a coin again." He turned to Jacob. "Get to it, coin master."

Jacob sighed as he took a quarter from his pocket and flipped it. "Heads!" Zach called before the coin had landed.

Jacob's face fell a little as he held it out. "Heads it is. You win."

So that was that, and even though a part of me agreed with Jacob and Emily's point, it was too late. It seemed I was guarding the shell.

I forced myself to stand tall again. I could do it. Right?

We walked back to the car. A guy a few years older than us was sitting in the front seat next to Violet. He had long blonde hair and stupid eyes and he and Violet were kissing like their lips had been glued together. As we reached the car, he leaped out and ran his fingers through his hair.

"You're back already?" Violet looked us up and down, clearly unimpressed with what she saw. "I thought you were fishing." Was that what Zach had told her? We weren't even carrying fishing rods!

"Oh, we got what we came for," Zach said, "now home please, Violet." He turned and looked at the guy she'd been kissing. He was busy fastening the strap of his motorcycle helmet as he strode to the bike parked behind Violet's car. "See you later, Dwayne."

Dwayne glanced back at Zach as if he wanted to crush him under his wheels. Then he climbed onto the seat, flicked his hair from his shoulders and sped away.

Violet drove us all back to their house, and I collected my bike and rode it home. The evening sky was blue, and butterflies flitted across the meadow as I raced up the track, the shell thumping in my hoody's pocket.

It had been a seriously weird day. Thinking about what a close call we'd had with the pirates at Baby Island rattled me, even though I hadn't let it get to me at the time. I'd managed to stay calm, which was how I'd saved Zach. As I realized that, I felt like I was on top of the world, or at least near its summit.

Then, as I got into the woods, a strange, ominous feeling shot through my stomach, like danger was close and it seemed as if the very trees were watching me.

I should have cycled faster, but I didn't.

And as I neared the house, the branches at the corner of our driveway rustled and two figures sprang out.

22

GRIMDIRES THROUGH AND
THROUGH

I t was the strangers.

I froze as the woman pulled a rifle out from under her long coat and the man brandished a shovel. Both looked as mean and dangerous as sharks.

"Give us the shell!" The woman's voice was shrill and scratchy, like fingernails screeching on a chalkboard. "Now!"

I shook my head. "I don't know what you're talking-"

"We saw you on Baby Island." The man was gruff and winded. He sounded like he'd been running for miles.

"How?" I asked.

"We followed you, boy," the woman said.

"We've been watching," the man added.

The woman pulled a battered old spyglass from her coat pocket. "I spy with my little eye..." She grinned, pleased with herself.

"Now." The man raised his shovel like an ax. It was caked in dry mud, at least I hoped it was mud. "Let's see what you've got."

"I haven't got anything," I lied, "apart from pocket lint. You can have that if you want. Maybe you can use it to make a new sweater." I forced myself to stand tall as I tried to wheel my bike past them. "I need to get h-"

"Give me the shell. We know you have it!" the woman said.

I remembered the glint of light as we'd set out along the beach. It must have been the sunlight reflecting off her telescope, which meant they'd seen *everything*. At least until the creepy mist rolled in.

"We want the map too," the man said, "quick smart!"

"I don't have it," I said, "Grimdire and his men showed up..."

"Oh we saw them," the man replied, "just like we saw you parading around with the map and shell."

"Well, Grimdire has it now," I said, "the parrot snatched it from me when I was helping my friend." I looked them square in the eyes.

The woman studied me for a moment before nodding. "I believe him, Fitzroy," she said, and then clapped a hand over her mouth.

"What did I tell you about using our real names, Angelina?" Fitzroy asked. And then he looked down at his filthy shoes. "I see what I did there..."

"Doesn't matter," Angelina said, "because if this repulsive child doesn't hand over that shell he'll be six feet under before nightfall." She cast a threatening glance at my house and raised her rifle. "Now, give me it!"

My fingers felt swollen as I reached into the pocket of my hoody and removed it. I felt sick. Jacob and Emily had been right; I shouldn't have taken the shell. I'd sworn to protect it day and night but I hadn't even made it home, and it was already slipping from my fingers.

Fitzroy snatched the shell and held it before his piggy eyes. "Oh, you ugly beauty!" He said. "We'll see what the invincible Captain Grimdire thinks about this!"

"But not until after we've salvaged the treasure from the Blight," Angelina added.

"Of course," Fitzroy said, "once we have that, we can send our dear old ancestor to his doom."

"Ancestor?" I asked before I could stop myself.

"Oh yes," Fitzroy said, "we're Grimdires through and through."

"On our sweet bony mother's side," Angelina added.

"But Captain Grimdire has had his day. This is the twenty first century" Fitzroy said, "and our birthright. We're going to be filthy stinking rich!"

They were already filthy and stinking, I thought, that was for sure, but I kept my mouth shut.

"Now, where's the Blight?" Angelina demanded, "we saw you studying the map after you plucked it from the chest. Where is it?"

"I don't know, I only saw it for a second." Her eyes were getting narrower and narrower like she was reading my lies. I needed to throw her a bone. "All I saw was an X and Zach said it was on Penn Cove."

"Where exactly?" Fitzroy growled. He brandished the spade inches from my face. It didn't smell so good.

"I don't know, somewhere in the middle I think."

"We don't need the exact spot. The pirates will lead us to it," Angelina said.

"True." Fitzroy's fingers sank into his fake beard and he began to scratch. Then he pulled something out, crushed it between his fingernails and gazed back to me. "So what do we do with this one?"

"Shoot him?" Angelina asked. "Or knock him upside the head with that shovel as many times as it takes?"

"Yes, we should croak him," Fitzroy said, "or," he thrust his face into mine until our noses almost touched, "maybe we could just let him go. Do you want us to let you go?"

I nodded quickly.

"Will you keep your mouth shut and stay out of our business?" Fitzroy said, "You, and your stupid friends? Because if you don't, we'll come calling. In the middle of the night. Understand?"

His breath smelt worse than canned cat food and I had to force myself not to gag. "I understand."

"Good." Angelina rested the rifle against her shoulder. "Come tomorrow you'll never see us again. You'd like that, wouldn't you?"

I nodded again.

"Then we have an agreement," Fitzroy said, "stay out of our way, keep your tongue still, and that'll be the end of it. Capish?"

I nodded. I understood.

They turned and wandered into the woods. I stayed where I was, rooted to the ground until I heard the last of their bumbling crashes.

Then I let out the breath I hadn't realized I'd been holding and stared into the trees, defeated. I'd messed up, big time. It was all my fault. Now the pirates had the map, and the maniacs had the shell. Which meant The Rotten Blight was about to rise, and so was that hideous, gigantic octopus.

"Well done, Dyllyboo," I said as I wheeled my bike back home.

"WHAT'S WRONG WITH YOUR FACE," JAMIE SAID, AS WE ATE dinner that night. Mom and Dad were in the living room watching TV, and he'd started taking shots at me as soon as they'd gotten up from the table. "You look like you want the ground to swallow you up. We've got that in common at least. What happened, did your wittle fwends give you the boot?"

"Shut up!" I shouted spearing the last bite of my chicken like it was his heart.

"Loser," he said as he slid his plate under the table and fed Wilson the rest of his dinner. Wilson stared at him lovingly, tail wagging. Even he wasn't on my side anymore.

I grabbed my plate, washed up the dishes and said goodnight to Mom and Dad before going up to my room. I thought about calling Zach, Emily, or Jacob and explaining what had happened, but I couldn't bring myself to do it. I'd failed. They wouldn't want to know me, not anymore. Jamie was right; I *was* a loser and a coward too. I tried to read a book, but my eyes just skimmed over the words.

Then I opened my battered laptop to play a game, but it crashed. So I switched the light off, curled onto my side, and stared at the wall, my worried thoughts turning in circles until I fell asleep.

23

GREY GLOOM

I woke from the worst dreams. My blankets were tangled on the floor, my pillows were crumpled up like I'd been punching them, and my hair was a wild spiky mess.

It took a moment for me to remember everything that had happened. The battle of Baby Island, the parrot snatching the map away and then the strangers stealing the shell...

"Idiot," I said.

The morning was as grey and gloomy as my thoughts. I glanced through the curtains and a scrawny deer gazed back until a distant boom echoed through the trees. It was the Fourth of July. Someone was already setting off fireworks. They probably couldn't wait for it to get dark tonight but I certainly could, because I knew that by midnight, either Fitzroy and Angelina would raise The Rotten Blight, or Captain Grimdire would.

I felt sick imagining the destruction that would happen when they did. And it was all my fault.

Rain spattered the window. How could it be so cold and gloomy, it was supposed to be summer? I didn't know what to do, so I slunk back into bed and pulled the blankets over my head because it was the best idea I could come up with.

Someone rapped on the door and I jumped. "What do you want?" I asked. I was pretty sure it was Jamie with some kind of stupid prank to make me feel even worse than I already did.

Dad opened the door with a big cheesy grin on his face. "Good morning, to you too," he said as he held his hands behind his back. "Happy Fourth of July!"

I forced a smile. "Happy Fourth of July."

"Guess what I've got?"

I shrugged. Unless it was the moon snail shell, I wasn't interested.

"Ta-da!" He threw a padded envelope to me.

I tore it open, confused. Inside was a charger for my phone. "Awesome!"

"Mom said she took you all over creation looking for one and I just know how much you love shopping! I figured you must have wanted it pretty badly so I ordered one online to spare you from any more expeditions and midnight garage sales."

"Thanks, Dad!" I said and gave him a hug.

"No problem, Dylan. Now, the weather's looking pretty grim this morning, but it's supposed to clear up later. Are you ready for some fireworks?"

"Sure." I forced another smile. There'd be fireworks tonight alright, but not the kind he was expecting to see.

"Good." He winked and left the room.

I plugged my phone in and a minute later the charging symbol appeared. I waited a bit longer before unlocking it. I didn't have any messages at all, not even a text. I was hoping I might have at least heard from Sam or Caden. I felt so alone, so I decided to call them.

Sam was out but Caden was home. We spoke for a while

and he asked a bunch of questions about the island. Talking to him felt weird, I couldn't tell him about all the stuff that had happened. There was no way he'd have believed any of it anyway and I couldn't blame him. So, it didn't take long for us to run out of things to say and that made me feel even worse. It had only been a week or so since I'd last seen him, but so much had changed, including me. "See you later, Caden," I said.

"Yeah, later."

I ended the call and thought about adding Jacob, Emily and Zach to my address book, but what was the point? I had a feeling our friendship was over, or would be just as soon as they found out what I'd done.

※

THE RAIN POURED ALL MORNING AND INTO THE AFTERNOON. Jamie was being his usual hyper-irritating self, so I went for a walk. It was wet and muddy and the huge puddles mirrored the dull grey sky.

I stopped at the end of our road. My hair, hoody and jeans were soaked through and as I gazed down I saw something moving in the puddle at my feet. It was an ant clinging to a twig, its tiny legs scurrying in the water like paddles.

The rain pummeled down but the ant kept fighting to steady itself. Before I could help it, it reached the edge and scurried off into the grass.

"I can't give up," I said out loud. Then I glanced around to make sure no one had heard me talking to myself. But I was alone; it was just me and the rain.

I ran all the way back to my house. Wheels turned in my mind. I had to do something, anything... I *had* to get the shell back. But how?

And then I remembered what Jacob had said before, about how he'd seen the strangers going into the woods just down the road from Zach and Emily's house. It wasn't far... If I rode fast I could get there in fifteen minutes. There was no guarantee the shell would be there, but I had to try something.

The phone inside the house rang as I grabbed my bike from the yard, wiped the seat down and took off. I heard Dad calling my name before I reached the end of the driveway, but I kept going. It was probably just Sam returning my call and I didn't have time to talk to him. I had things to do.

The wind blew and the rain fell harder, spattering me like glassy bullets. Soon I was forced to take shelter under a tree.

I was cold and drenched. All I wanted to do was turn around, go home, take a hot shower and forget about everything.

Then I thought about what Gillian Tweedle had told us. Of how Grimdire wanted his revenge, of how he'd sworn to destroy the island. How could I live with myself, knowing that was coming? Thoughts raced through my mind, chasing each other like dogs. Angelina and Fitzroy had said they'd kill me if I interfered in their business; they'd been very clear about that.

The rain lightened up a little so I set out again. The roads were weirdly quiet on the outskirts of town and the lack of traffic and people began to freak me out. I almost turned back and headed home. Almost. Instead I thought about the ant. Of how it had held on no matter what, even though it must have felt like the world was crashing down around it. "I have to be the ant," I said as I pounded the pedals as fast as they'd go.

The trees along the road grew thicker and I slowed as I spotted the trail heading into the shadowy woods. My tires rumbled as I started down the potholed track. A moment later the sky vanished as the branches drew over me like a tunnel. Suddenly it hit me; where I was, what I was about to do and icy terror gnawed at my resolve.

I desperately wanted to turn back, and I was about to when something splashed through the puddle behind me.

Someone was there!

I wanted to look but I panicked. Instead of turning, I cycled faster and faster but whoever was behind me was rattling ever closer.

24

THE MEANEST, DUMBEST IDEA
EVER!

"**D**ylan!"

It was Jacob. I turned as he caught up with me. Emily and Zach trailed just behind him.

I felt massive relief followed by heavy confusion. "What are you guys doing here?"

"We called your house," Jacob said as the others braked behind him. "Your dad said you'd just taken off on your bike. It was pouring down with rain so we knew something was up. Then Emily spotted you down the road, and it's a good thing she did." He looked around and shook his head. "I told you I saw those strangers coming down this way, don't you remember?"

"Fitzroy and Angelina," I said.

"You know their names!" Emily asked, "Did something happen?"

I nodded slowly. I felt ashamed, and then angry. I wanted to tell them but at the same time, I really didn't. The two thoughts went to war inside my head until finally, I blurted it all out.

"Oh, that's not good," Zach said.

My face felt hot, like it must be glowing like a lamp. There was no way to hide my embarrassment, I just had to bear it. And then Zach added, "But I'd have done the same if they'd come after me with a shovel."

"And a rifle," I said.

"Yeah, me too," Emily agreed.

"Yep," Jacob said, "I'd have handed over the shell the moment I saw them. It sounds like you held out for as long as you could. Good for you, but..." He paused as a stern expression crossed his face. "You shouldn't have come out here on your own."

"No," Emily agreed, "we're your friends, Dylan. You can trust us."

"Mostly," Zach added with a grin.

I nodded. I couldn't remember feeling so relieved. I'd been so sure they were going to hate me for losing the shell. "Can you help me get it back?" I asked.

"Sure," Emily said.

"Great!" I said, but as I glanced into the trees a dose of walloping fear snaked through me. There might have been four of us but Angelina and Fitzroy were armed, and we were alone in the woods with them.

"Wait!" Jacob rode up the trail for a moment before skidding to a halt. "Nice," he said, as he peered around the bend in the track. "That could work!"

We followed him to where someone had dumped a bunch of trash by the side of the path. It was mostly clothes; odd socks, a torn sweater and a pair of long johns. There was also a half burnt mattress and lots and lots of empty tin cans.

"What a mess. I bet they did it," Emily said, "they're exactly the kind of people who'd do something like this."

"Yep," Zach said, "dumpers!"

"Yeah," I agreed, "I could imagine Fitzroy wearing those long johns."

"They're perfect!" Jacob said as he examined the trash. And then he adjusted his glasses and glanced at each of us in turn. "I've got a plan."

"No way!" Zach shook his head so hard his hair flew up around him.

"You lost the coin toss," Emily said.

"And I'm the coin master, remember?" Jacob asked.

"That's an abuse of power! I'm the one that granted you that title, remember?" Zach said, "don't use your prestige against me, it's not fair!"

"You called tails, you lost fair and square," Jacob said.

"But I lost the last one too!" Zach protested.

"So?" Emily asked.

"Yeah, that's a separate issue," Jacob said, "now get on with it."

"I'm going to smell like old man socks now. For months!" Zach swore as he stooped and picked up the long johns. His face twisted with disgust as he examined them before slowly pulling them up over his jeans. "Gross!" Next, he put on the tattered coat, which was torn up one side.

Jacob pulled a length of twine from his backpack and tied it around Zach's waist, holding everything in place. "Now go, make like a pig," he said as he pointed at the ground.

"This is the meanest, dumbest idea ever," Zach said as he rolled across the muddy trail, covering himself in filth.

"Here!" Emily returned from the trees with clumps of moss. She used the twine to secure them around his head. Then, with the last bit of the string, Jacob tied the tin cans to the back of his coat. They clattered and rattled as Zach strutted around like an irritable peacock.

"This better work," Zach said.

I hoped it would too because if it didn't, there was a big chance at least one of us would be shot before the day was over. And most likely that someone would be me.

We carried the tin cans behind Zach and followed a snaking trail to an old shack that was half hidden in a wooded hollow.

The place was a wreck. Its shattered windows were strung with milky-blue spider webs and the old boarded walls were caked in moss and mildew. A fire burned inside sending an orange glow over one of the windows as smoke belched from the wonky chimney.

"That doesn't look totally creepy," I said, shaking my head.

"Imagine how many bugs are crawling around in there," Zach said with disgust. "At least a billion. Maybe even a trillion!"

Emily looked seriously worried as she studied me. "Are you sure you want to do this, Dylan?"

"No," I said, "but I have to, right?"

Zach nodded. "If we're going to try and stop Grimdire from destroying the entire island and taking thousands of lives, then yeah."

"Sneak around to the back door. It won't give you any trouble; someone kicked it in awhile back so the lock's broken," Jacob said. "We'll keep them occupied out here."

"Right," I said, forcing a bravery I wasn't quite feeling. I moved through the trees, keeping low.

I was almost at the rear of the shack when someone passed by the orange-lit window. Fitzroy. I could hear him muttering to himself. I wanted to race back to the path, grab my bike, and pedal like crazy until I was home. I came close, but as I glanced back to the others, I knew I couldn't let them down.

"You can do this," I whispered as I headed down the incline. I stepped carefully through the brush, avoiding the twigs and branches, creeping like I hoped a ninja might. "Be the ant."

Pure will kept me going until a muffled explosion roared through the woods behind me.

✤ 25 ✤

SCURVY SAILORS

Zach stumbled out from the trees trailed by swirls of thick white smoke. Someone must have brought some smoke bombs from their Fourth of July stash. My money was on Jacob.

The tin cans rattled as Zach lumbered toward the shack, and then a pirate-like voice growled from behind him. It was loud and tinny, like some kind of recording. It blared, "Arrr, me scurvy sailors!"

I could see Emily tucked behind a tree holding out Jacob's phone. The voice was followed by the cry of seagulls and then it started again, "Arrr me scurvy sailors!" like it was on a loop.

Thud!

The front door flew open and Fitzroy blundered out, followed by Angelina. They clutched shovels and at first, they looked angry, then afraid. They slowed as they glanced over at Zach. He must have looked pretty strange from where they stood because neither of them seemed to want to go any closer.

Another smoke bomb hissed and Fitzroy cowered. "Wha... what do you want?" he pleaded.

"We haven't done anything wrong," Angelina added, "not yet."

"And we won't," Fitzroy said. "Your master, the right honorable Captain Grimdire, is our kin. We'd never do anything to cause him harm."

"Arrr, me scurvy sailors!"

They stepped back and lowered their shovels.

I hurried through the trees until I reached the back of the cabin. The door was broken, just as Jacob had said. Someone had tried to tie it shut with an old stocking but it only took a second to unhook it and slip through.

The place was even filthier inside than I'd imagined. It was dark and gloomy and stank of rot. There were old brown bottles everywhere and someone had strung a net of fairy lights from the ceiling and attached them to a car battery. At first, I thought they were twinkling on purpose, and then I realized they were shorting out.

A heavy scent of oil came from the old-fashioned lamps and their light flickered across the rotten floorboards and wooden crates. I stepped over piles of dusty trash bags limply stuffed with clothes and paused by a rickety table. It was covered in maps, chipped dirty cups and notebooks scrawled with tiny, angry-looking writing.

Then, I saw the newspaper clipping that was fastened to the wall with a bread knife. There was a picture of a stony faced policewoman and someone had added a devilish beard, horns and round glasses over her eyes with a black marker. The headline read:

'Burglary At The Much Beloved Three Rocks Museum! Criminal Siblings Sought!'

I glanced over the story. Apparently thieves had broken into a small museum in a town outside Seattle and journals belonging to a sailor, who was rumored to be a pirate, had been stolen. They didn't mention his name, but it had to be related to Grimdire. The article said the police were searching for Fitzroy and Angelina Strimple; a brother and sister team with a long history of criminal behavior.

Their picture was at the bottom of the article. They looked different, Fitzroy wasn't sporting his fake beard and Angelina was without her glasses and coat, but I still recognized them, their ratty faces and mean jagged teeth were totally distinctive.

"Where, where, where?" I muttered as I glanced around the shack, hoping to find the shell. There was no sign of it. It could have been anywhere, buried under their heaps of trash, or stashed in one of their pockets for all I knew.

Then I spotted Angelina's beret resting on an old dresser and peeking out from beneath it a pearly gleam that shone in the lamp light. The shell!

I took a deep breath and crept across the creaky floor.

Outside, the Strimples were still and frozen as they watched Zach inch toward them. He was still shrouded in the misty white smoke, but it was thinning. They must have run out of smoke bombs.

"Arrr, me scurvy sailors!" The voice blared again.

The shovels in the Strimples hands rose as they turned and whispered to each other. Time was running out. I needed to distract them so my friends could get away, but first the shell... I almost had it when my sneaker burst through the rotten floor.

Crunch!

I was about to free myself when a high-pitched squeak came from the hole and something brushed against my leg. As it crept across my foot I felt warm fur against my bare ankle. A shriek burst from my mouth as I tried to wrench my foot free.

I grabbed hold of a chair to steady myself as the shack door flew open with an almighty crash.

❧ 26 ❧

THE STRIMPLES

The Strimples appeared just as I yanked my foot from the hole. Somehow they'd gotten stuck in the doorway in a tangle of limbs.

I stumbled to the dresser and grabbed the shell from under Angelina's beret.

"You!" she cried, as she freed herself and burst into the room.

Fitzroy shoved her aside and bounded past her. "Give me that shell or I'll pulverize you!"

I ran for the back door. Something whooshed through the air. I ducked as a shovel struck the wall and bit into the wood.

"Damn its eyes!" Fitzroy barked. I didn't know if he was cursing me, the shovel or the shack. I staggered and dodged aside as I heard another whoosh!

Thang! The other shovel hit the door exactly where my head had been. "Demon child!" Angelina cried. "Come back here, now!"

"Like that's going to happen!" I shouted as I flung the door open. I glanced over my shoulder as Fitzroy's leg slipped through the hole I'd made. His sister stumbled into him with such force she flew head over heels and landed in a heap of trash.

I ran up the rise toward the trees. Emily was a few yards ahead of me, running as fast as she could. Zach was too, his tin cans scraping and bouncing off stones and fallen branches.

Jacob was there waving us on. "Run!" He shouted as he grabbed my shoulder and propelled me on. We sprinted hard, flying through the trees, our breaths panicked.

We watched as pieces of Zach's outfit were flung into the air, one by one, and followed the trail strewn behind him on the muddy ground. First the rope, then the old coat and the strung up cans. After some crazed hopping he shed the long johns then flung his mossy headdress into the dirt. He and Emily jumped on their bikes and turned as we raced toward them. "Hurry!" Emily cried.

I didn't need to look. I could hear the Strimples; they were right on our heels and filling the air with curses and threats. I grabbed my handlebars, yanked my bike off the ground and ran, leaping onto the seat as Jacob matched my every move.

"Go!" Zach cried as he stood on his pedals and pumped like mad.

My bike wobbled crazily, and the trees became a blur. The others were ahead, Zach leading, then Emily, then Jacob who had somehow overtaken me. Our tires hit holes and stones, slowing us down. We bounced along on our seats as Jacobs phone went off, shouting, "Arrr, me scurvy sailors!"

"Come here, boy!" Fitzroy was right behind me, his hand reaching for my hoody.

With a sudden burst, I pedaled harder than I'd ever pedaled and was finally out of his reach.

"This way!" Jacob called. They'd left the trail and sped

through the trees, their wheels whirring, their frames clanking.

I shot along the trail after them, skidding left and right to zip through the woods as the Strimples stomped behind me. They sounded further away now.

Zach and Emily vanished and a moment later Jacob leaped his bike over the top of the slope and vanished too. I jumped, taking my bike with me.

I flew for a moment, sailed down and struck the spongy earth with both wheels before shooting down a ditch and zipping up onto a road. I followed the others as the spray from their wheels misted the air and soaked my face. I didn't care, I was just glad to be alive.

WE PULLED UP BY EMILY AND ZACH'S PLACE.

"The tree house," Zach said, "now!"

"We need to stash our bikes," Jacob said, "in case they come looking for us."

"They'll probably go to my house, they know where I live," I said with a sinking feeling. "Maybe I should warn Mom and Dad."

"I don't think the Strimples would do anything that bold," Emily said, "they seem like cowards to me."

"What kind of name is Strimple anyway?" Zach grinned, and then he used Strimple at least twenty times in a variety of stupid voices. I laughed, even though I was still pretty freaked out.

"They're actually wanted criminals." I told them about the newspaper clipping as we hid our bikes behind the garden shed and climbed the ladder to the tree house.

"That's probably why they're wearing those disguises," Jacob said.

Emily pulled her phone out. "We should call the police."

"And tell them what? That the Strimples are out to steal some buried treasure that's the rightful property of undead pirates?" Zach asked. "Those fools are probably long gone by now anyway and we'll get busted for filing a false report. It happens all the time."

"In Langley?" I asked.

"No, on the shows I watch, but... look, it'd be great if we could tell some adults what's going on and let them deal with it, but they're never going to believe us, are they? Best case scenario, we'll get grounded and placed under house arrest, and that's the last thing we need right now!"

"So what are we going to do?" Emily asked. "According to the legend, tonight's Grimdire's last chance to raise The Rotten Blight. He has the map. There's no way he's going to waste this opportunity and wait another fifty years!"

"We've got the shell now," Jacob said, "we'll have to use it and summon the octopus. It's the only way we can take down Grimdire and his men. Once they're out of the way we can go to the police and report the Strimples. They're already looking for them and this way we won't need to mention the pirates."

Emily agreed, "Grimdire's got the map, so we know he'll be on the cove. The Strimples too."

"Right where X marks the spot," Jacob said, bringing up the scan of the map on his phone.

"At midnight," I added.

"Right," Zach said, "which means we'll need to be there too. But how?" He paced around the top of the tree house, brushing his hair back and forth with his hand until it looked like someone had rubbed a balloon over his head. And then he gave an evil grin. "Violet. She'll take us."

"No, she's going to Seattle," Emily said, "remember?"

"Not anymore she's not," Zach said, "I've still got plenty of intel. Stuff she doesn't even know that I know. She'll bend to my will. And don't feel sorry for her, Em. She'd strike like a crazed cobra if she had dirt on us. And that's what she is; a cobra in a skin suit." He turned to Jacob. "Does your dad still have that boat?"

"Yep, and he's been going crabbing a lot so it's already out there on the cove. It's a ways from where the X is on the map but we can easily get it over to the right spot."

"What kind of boat is it?" I asked, trying to sound casual. The thought of being on the open water made me feel sick, especially at midnight with a bunch of zombie pirates lurking there. But a speedboat or yacht might be okay and there was always-

"It's a rowboat," Jacob said, stopping my thoughts dead.

Great.

"Now," he continued, pointing at Zach and Emily, "you two go and do whatever you have to do to get Violet on board. And then ask your parents if you can come and watch the fireworks with me tonight. I'll ask mine if I can go watch them with you guys, they should be okay with that. Dylan, you should probably do the same."

Emily, Zach and Jacob disappeared down the ladder as I sat back on the hammock and called home. No one answered.

As I hung up, I laid back and gazed out at the sky. There were some patches of blue but it was mostly gray, and the gloom was making everything feel ominous. Fear jabbed through me as I considered what we were about to do. The more I thought about it, the crazier it seemed. Would tonight be my last night on earth? It was starting to feel that way.

"Done," Jacob called up from below. A few minutes later there was a crash inside the house and some yelling. Then Emily and Zach came out smiling as they flashed us the thumbs up sign.

It was on.

I forced a smile and climbed down the ladder. The others looked scared but excited. I wished I was. "I called but no one was home," I said. "It's probably better if I ask them face-to-face, anyway. Mom hasn't met you guys yet, and she can be pretty cautious. So..." Suddenly I was starting to see a way out. Even though it was wrong...

"Go home and call me as soon as they get back," Emily said. "I'll come over and you can ask your mom while I'm there so I can back up your story. It should be fine; people's mom's usually like me."

"About as much as they hate me," Zach added as he kicked a stone across the grass.

"Okay," I said. And with that, my plan to get myself out of this mess was officially nixed. I grabbed my bike and headed home under the darkening clouds, which felt about right.

༄

I FOUND DAD HAULING GROCERIES OUT OF THE CAR AS I pulled up. "Feeling better?" he asked.

"Sure."

"Did your friends find you? They called just as you left."

"Yeah, I met up with them just down the road." I carefully laid my bike down, instead of dropping it like I usually did. I wasn't looking for a lecture, I needed to keep things sweet. "Hey," I asked, "have you seen anyone out in the woods?"

"What do you mean?"

"Like, I don't know." How could I tell him about the Strimples without worrying him? That was the last thing I needed. I shrugged.

"No lurkers," he smiled, "but a nice couple came calling earlier."

"Oh?"

"Yes, Frederick's parents. They were looking for him and wondered if he was hanging out with you."

Frederick. Surely a name only a Strimple would make up. "Oh, a bunch of us went riding all around," I said. "He's probably back home by now." I hated being sneaky. I wanted to tell him everything but I had to stay off his radar if I didn't want to be on lockdown for the rest of the week.

"Good. I'm glad you're making friends, Dylan. I know that was one of your biggest worries when we told you we were moving."

I nodded and grabbed a couple of bags, lifting them up high as Wilson tried to sniff them. Then Mom called us in for lunch so I texted Emily real quick and sat down to eat. Jamie wasn't home so it was nice and peaceful. I listened as they talked about weeding the garden, then Emily knocked on the door just as we were finishing our cherry pie.

She was right, Mom started fawning over her immediately and Dad seemed really happy to meet her too. They asked her a million questions and Emily answered them all and smiled a lot. If it had been a test she'd have gotten an A+. I was really glad she'd come over, and even gladder that Zach had stayed home.

And then, once she had them eating out of her hands, she asked them if I could go with her and Zach to watch the fireworks and camp out with them overnight in their back yard.

Mom agreed right away but Dad seemed disappointed that I wouldn't be celebrating at home with them. I decided I'd make it up to him later, and suggested a special Fifth of July barbecue to celebrate our move. He seemed happy with that, although there was the question of whether I'd even be alive by then, not that I mentioned it.

Before I knew it we were on our bikes racing toward Langley, a breeze sweeping over our heads as it chased the clouds away.

It was happening.

The mission was on.

🦋 27 🦋

THE INTREPID GUPPY

It was ten at night by the time we got to Coupeville and it was getting dark. Zach and Emily's folks had gone out early, probably to see the same fireworks show my parents were going to, which had given us time to plan.

Violet glared at us in her rearview mirror. "I swear this is the last time I'm doing this, Zach, so you'd better live it up."

"We'll see, Vi," he said as we hopped out of the car. A moment later there was a rumble and Violet's boyfriend turned up on his motorbike. He took his helmet off and shook his hair free as if he was starring in a shampoo commercial. Then he gave each of us a look. I got the feeling he hated us too.

"Cool. It looks like Vi won't have time to spy on us," Zach said as we walked down toward the cove. The sky was a deep blackish blue and fireworks whizzed and crackled like burning pips before bursting into red and green blossoms.

We could see the town of Coupeville across the still dark water of the cove. It seemed so far away. There was no sign of Grimdire or the Strimples but I had a feeling that was about to change, and soon.

Jacob led us to a cluster of rowboats that were chained

together on the stony beach. His dad's boat looked like it had at least fifty coats of paint on it and all the previous colors peeked out in the places where the newer layers had chipped or peeled away. The name on the side read:

'The Intrepid Guppy'.

"Dad thought it was funny," Jacob explained as he unlocked the padlock and turned to hand out the life jackets stowed beneath the benches. There was one for each of us and two to spare.

We lifted the boat and dragged it to the water, setting it down several times to give our aching arms a rest. Then, at Jacob's say-so, we pushed it out onto the cove. Everyone else jumped on as I watched the whole boat wobble like crazy. Then they turned back and looked at me as I stood on the shore, gazing stupidly back at them, my stomach rolling.

"Come on, Dylan, what are you waiting for?" Zach called.

Emily offered a hand to help me but I leaped into the boat without taking it and shut my eyes as it rocked all over the place.

"You alright?" Jacob asked.

"Sure," I lied. "What time is it?" I asked as if I wasn't completely and utterly terrified.

"Almost eleven," Jacob said, "so we've got an hour. We should practice rowing."

"I know how to row," Zach said.

"Well I don't," I said. My nerves were fried.

We paddled along the shore and slowly I got into the rhythm as Jacob sat at the front, training us. There was still plenty of time until midnight so we moored up and took a break.

Soon, Zach had us laughing with his ridiculous *facts* and exaggerations while fireworks painted the sky and the wispy haze of gunpowder smoke drifted through the air. I almost forgot why we were there, and as Jacob cracked a joke, making us all laugh again, I realized I couldn't remember being happier than I was in that moment.

And then...

"Look!" Emily pointed across the cove. My heart sank as I followed her finger.

A growing column of chalky-blue fog rolled across the water from the east.

Grimdire.

Soon the fog blended with the sulfurous smoke and it seemed the entire cove was smothered in mist.

"Give me the shell," Emily said gravely.

"Are you sure?" Jacob asked as he pulled it from his backpack.

"I'm the best swimmer," she said, "and one of us needs to get to The Rotten Blight without them seeing us. That way we can lead the octopus right to them."

I shuddered. She had no idea how big the creature was but I'd actually seen it. I wanted to spring from the boat and run back to Violet's car, but I forced myself to stay where I was.

"Just keep the boat nearby, right?" Emily's voice was calm but there was a glimmer of fear in her eyes.

I nodded, but what I should have done was offer to take the shell myself. After all, I was the one that had lost the map. But the thought of diving into the water sent an icy shiver down my spine so I watched in silence as Emily took the shell.

"Ready?" Jacob asked. His face was grave. We nodded. "Right, row then," he said as he perched at the front and gazed out across the water.

We took up the oars and slowly but surely paddled toward the smoke sailing across the cold, black inky water.

❧ 28 ❧

MIDNIGHT ON THE COVE

A chill swept over the cove along with the peppery smell of gunpowder snaking through the murky damp fog. I jumped as another roaring volley of fireworks exploded above us. They'd looked so pretty earlier, but now they filled me with dread. Everything was starting to feel like a scene from a horror movie.

The image of the octopus squirmed through my mind as we rowed through the blackness; its horrible size paired with that terrible, scarred face and those lamp-like milky eyes. What if it mistook us for Grimdire? What if it didn't care whose side we were on? What if it just saw us all as tasty meat snacks?

Did octopus' eat people? Were they carnivores?

My hands trembled so I gripped the oars harder, determined not to show my rising terror. The mist grew thicker, its edges swirling like grey tentacles. A low groan of boards came from the darkness followed by the tortured creak of ropes.

Another round of fireworks burst above us, illuminating the pirate ship hidden in the fog as the booming explosions echoed along the cove like thunder. I caught a glimpse of Grimdire standing at the bow gazing down into the water. He raised his cutlass. A moment later there was a heavy splash and a loud wooden groan as the vessel ground to a stuttering halt.

"They dropped anchor," Jacob whispered.

The twinkling light of the fireworks faded and everything turned black.

"Did... did you see them?" Zach's voice was so quiet I almost didn't hear him.

"Yes," Emily whispered.

"Paddle slowly," Jacob said, "keep her steady."

"Do you think I should go now?" Emily asked. She sounded casual like it was no big thing. My heart swelled with admiration and I wished I had just a scrap of her bravery. "Or should we wait for them to raise the-"

Beep!

Jacob seized his wristwatch and thumbed the alarm off. "Sorry," he said, looking embarrassed. "That means it's midnight."

Another firework went off. Grimdire held the blade of his cutlass to the palm of his hand as he stood at the gunwale, then he made a quick cutting motion.

We watched in stunned silence as bright glowing green drops fell into the water.

"It's his blood!" Zach whispered. He sounded fascinated and horrified at the same time. An eerie glow lit the inky black waves.

"He's raising The Rotten Blight!" Emily whispered.

My heart pounded as a long creak echoed up from below. Then a heavy wrenching sound rang out as millions of bubbles rose to the surface, bringing the stench of rot and ash.

"Back up! Paddle, move us away," Jacob hissed, pointing

toward the shoreline. Our arms shook as we rowed toward the edge of the mist and away from the swirling water.

Another blast of fireworks thundered overhead, punctuating the hiss of the bubbles and the groaning rise of the ship.

All of us gasped as a long dark mast with a sopping black flag broke the surface. It was followed by the crow's nest, foremast, booms and shrouds. Soon the massive hull burst from the water and cresting waves broke along the cove. Our boat rocked and bucked but we held on tight, riding it out, each of us silent despite our terror.

The Rotten Blight dwarfed Grimdire's pilfered ship. It was a towering, putrid galleon that seemed to tower so high up into the night the tip of its mast might have pierced the stars. At least that's how it seemed in that terrifying moment.

As it pitched and rolled on the waves the carved figurehead of a giant medusa stared balefully across the cove with dead white eyes and the twinkling fireworks continued to rain down around us. For a moment it seemed her eyes may have blinked as her serpent hair writhed in the mist.

I felt sick as soon as I saw the cannons jutting from the gun ports along the side of the ship. They hadn't even rusted. The ship had sunk so long ago, which meant it should have been as rotten as its name but it wasn't. The cannons were as fresh and deadly as the day Grimdire had seized them and their sheer size and number made me feel like a sitting duck. The Rotten Blight was a mobile weapon poised to destroy everything within its reach. I'd never seen anything so chilling in my life.

"We've got to take it down," I said, even though the thought of battling the galleon from our little boat was terrifying.

"Look!" Jacob pointed at the silhouettes of Grimdire and

his men as they climbed the rigging of their ship. Then they swung from the long ropes and leaped onto the deck of The Rotten Blight with soft, steady thuds.

"Use the shell, now" Zach hissed, "we're close enough!"

"No!" Jacob held out a trembling hand. "If that octopus is as big as Dylan said, and I believe it is, it'll take us down right along with the Blight. Emily, if you're going to swim over there then you need to do it now. We'll circle around the ship. The shell should draw the beast to the Blight. Once you've summoned it, dive off and we'll all row back to shore. Hopefully, that'll be the end of it."

"And if it isn't?" I asked.

Jacob gazed at The Rotten Blight. "Then I guess we're all fish food."

"Don't worry, I can do this," Emily said as she stood. I heard a tremble in her voice and saw the fear in her eyes. It was my second chance to set things right, or to at least go with her. But my deep, dark dread of the sea snagged me in its vicious tentacles and I held my tongue.

"Good luck, Em," Zach said.

"Watch for us, we'll be here," Jacob said as he seized one of the oars.

Emily gave a brief, brave smile, removed her lifejacket and lowered herself over the side. Her whole body seemed to shiver until she was submerged in the water.

She gripped the side of the boat with one hand and held the shell with the other. With a deep breath she nodded to us, turned and swam toward the Blight. Fireworks boomed all around, illuminating her in their glow and for a moment she was swimming sure and steady. But then she stopped.

Slowly, she turned, her face pinched with agony.

"What is it?" Zach cried.

For a terrible second I thought the octopus had her, but then she called, "Cramp! I can't move my leg!"

"Row!" Jacob pulled the oar furiously. Zach and I joined him. He hissed orders as we turned in circles. We righted our course and just as we glided toward her a clattering, choking sound rose up from behind us. I looked back, my heart racing.

A small, filthy tug boat was heading for the galleon. At the bow, clutching a rifle was Angelina Strimple. Her brother had his head out the window as he steered, his eyes glinting as a firework lit the night.

They hadn't seen us. I felt a jab of relief until they crossed our path in their quest for The Rotten Blight, cutting us off from Emily in a cloud of oily smoke.

Then her cries vanished.

29

DANCING THE HEMPEN JIG

"**G**o around them! Quick!" Jacob cried.

"It'll take too long!" Zach said, "she could be-"
His words trailed off into a desolate sob.

I jumped up, sending the boat wobbling madly and then before I could stop myself, I plunged into the cove. It was as black as coffee and icy cold.

Suddenly, I realized what I'd done. I was in the water!

The tug boat puttered toward The Rotten Blight, spewing a trail of filthy smoke. The bulky life jacket made it hard to move, but I kicked my legs hard and forced myself to swim, my hands pulling hard, my terror building fast. I refused to give into it. All that mattered was finding Em.

As I arced around the back of the tug, I saw her. She was chalky-white and her hands were flailing. If the Strimples had seen her, they'd left her to drown.

"You're okay!" I swam over and reached out to her. My fear vanished. All I cared about was helping her. She took my hands. "Can you tread water?" I asked. "You know how to do that, right?"

"Sure." Slowly the panic left her eyes and we waved our

arms through the water together until we heard the splash of oars behind us. I turned to find Jacob and Zach standing on the wobbling boat. Together they lifted Emily aboard, and I climbed in after her.

"Sorry," Emily said, as she clutched her shins. It looked like she was still in plenty of pain.

We glanced back at the galleon. Sailors scurried across the deck as Grimdire stood at the helm barking orders. They were loading the cannons, but it seemed they hadn't noticed the tug boat sputtering around them like a slow lazy bee.

"Give me the shell." Jacob held his hand out to Emily.

"You can't do it," Zach said, "you're the only one who knows how to row this boat."

"I'll go," I said. It was almost as if someone else had said it. But my hand was already reaching out and before I could stop myself, I was holding the shell.

My heart thumped as the others gaped at me. I gave what I hoped was a sure, confident nod and turned toward the water. Before I could think twice, I jumped back in and slipped down into the salty, freezing depths. I clutched the shell in one hand and used the other to swim. My arms and legs shook, either from the fear or the cold, I wasn't sure which.

The mist grew thicker as I swam toward The Rotten Blight. I was almost there when something brushed my leg and I was forced to swallow my cries.

Focus, I told myself. It was only a matter of time before Grimdire unleashed his cannons on the town. Who knew how many lives might be lost...

Then I heard the rope ladder clattering against the side of the ship. I swam toward it and grasped its wooden rungs. I thrust the shell into the pocket of my sodden hoody and pulled myself up out of the water.

Rung after rung I climbed, my arms aching, my legs trembling. Before I knew it I was up and onto the deck.

There were pirates everywhere; raising sails, climbing the rigging and swabbing the sea soaked deck. None of them seemed to notice as I crept toward the quarterdeck.

"Man the cannons port side," cried a heavy, booming voice. Grimdire. He stood in the dewy mist, his cutlass raised and pointing at Coupeville. "Let's paint the town red, boys!" he added, his voice full of spite.

I lifted the shell but before I could blow, someone gripped my arm. I turned to find a pirate standing behind me. He was dressed in a ragged black coat that blended in with the heavy gloom.

"Ye didn't see me, sonny boy, but I saw ye!" he cackled. His hand was icy and ghost-like, but its grip on my arm was solid. "This way!" He dragged me along the deck and into the lantern light. It seemed they could stand the light now they were back on their cursed galleon, and they were becoming more real by the moment.

"Look what I found, captain!" the pirate called. One by one the cursed crew turned and eyeballed me.

"Well, well, well," Grimdire said as he stared down with pitiless eyes. "A stowaway. And one of those treacherous children, no less." He turned to his crew. "Prepare a noose, so he can dance the hempen jig!"

"My pleasure," the pirate said as he released my arm, shoved me toward Grimdire, and pulled a length of rope from the deck.

I was going to die...

"Weigh anchor!" Grimdire called, "we'll hang this scurvy rat as we torch the town. It'll be the last thing he sees before he goes to his grave!"

A clattering din came from behind me as three pirates manned the levers of the capstan and began to turn it.

"The shell!" Grimdire's shadow fell over the lantern light like a thick black tattered cloak. "Give it now before I-" With a heavy splash the anchor rose from the cove and the boat rocked.

I feigned a left and took a right. Grimdire's hand swept toward me in what seemed to be slow motion. Before he could grab me I raised the shell and blew into it with everything I had.

A long shrill whistle burst from the shell and echoed along the cove like the howl of a gale force wind.

Grimdire shouted but I didn't hear his words as I dodged past and dropped the shell into his coat pocket. I didn't need it anymore, the ship was about to go down.

Or so I hoped...

Swish!

A pirate fumbled over to cut me off, and the hideous parrot balanced on his shoulder squawked. I grabbed the bird. It was ghostly and almost as thin as the air but there was enough of it for my fingers to grasp onto. It flapped and screamed as I threw it into the pirate's face.

Swish!

Grimdire's cutlass swept over my head.

I ducked and side-stepped, reaching for the sword thrust into the wooden rail before me. With a grunt, I pulled it free and circled as Grimdire lunged at me. Our blades locked and the blow was so great I struggled to keep my grip.

I'd never held a sword in my life and realizing that almost froze me with fear. And then I remembered every sword fight I'd ever watched in the movies and raised my cutlass with both hands to block his next attack.

Clang!

The force almost sent me reeling to the slick deck but somehow I stayed on my feet.

"C'mere boy!" Grimdire growled, "I'm going to pluck your heart out and feed it to the gulls!"

I ducked another swipe and raced to the back of the Blight. I leaped onto the rail and balanced there as I glanced over the edge, searching for Jacob and the others. The mist was too thick, the galleon was moving too fast and inky darkness loomed below me.

My heart hammered like a drum.

What choice was there? Stay and hang, or face the giant octopus?

At least if I jumped I might stand a chance...

I leaped.

Cold grasping fingers snatched my shoulders and I screamed as they yanked me back aboard the cursed ship.

30

A LEAP INTO DARKNESS

Captain Grimdire was looking far less ghostly as I gazed at his craggy face. He was more solid. More real. "It's time to pay the toll, boy," he growled, "and no amount of gold or pearls will suffice. No, you'll pay with your life for this treachery!"

He drew back his cutlass and slashed the strap of my life vest. I fell to the deck. He thrust his cutlass into the rail, then seized me with both hands and swung me out over the back of the ship. "I'd hang you, but the clock's ticking and that island needs to burn."

I glanced at the sheer darkness below and then to the approaching lights of Coupeville.

There was a chance I could make it to the shore, but I doubted it.

"Are you ready to visit Davy Jones' locker?" Grimdire's golden tooth flashed amongst the rotten dark stumps of his teeth.

"Drop dead!" I said.

"Indeed! I'll be doing that, boy. But not tonight!"

Grimdire held me in one fist and grabbed his cutlass in the other. "Let's see if you can swim without your hands!"

My scream caught in my throat.

Bang!

Something shot past Grimdire's head.

We both stared down at the approaching tug boat as Angelina Strimple took aim with her rifle. "Stop the ship and hand over your treasure! Now!" she cried.

"Shoot again and I'll scupper the boy!" Grimdire shouted back.

Angelina's laugh wafted up like a bad smell. "Be my guest, I'd consider that a bonus! Now give us our treasure or we'll grant you a second death!"

Grimdire shoved me onto the deck. It seemed I'd been cast aside now that he had a new foe to contend with. "Starboard!" he yelled.

The galleon groaned as it swung hard to the right. "We'll give you a treasure alright, you rotten dogs," he cried to the Strimples. "How about a nice shiny cannon ball?"

I could hear the artillery being loaded as the ship listed wildly. Terror rooted me to the deck until I saw the old red building at the end of the pier looming fast. The Blight would tear through it as if it were made of matchsticks. I ran, dodging cutlasses and sidestepping the blazing roar of ancient pistols. I dove below the mainsail and evaded a leering pirate who charged at me with a plank of wood.

The galleon listed and rocked, tossing me around like a puppet. I glanced over the side, searching for Jacob and the others, my heart racing harder than ever.

There was no sign of them. All I could see was pitch black water amid the fog.

And then a voice rose from the mist. "Dylan!"

A faint light waved through the air. It had to be from Jacob's phone. They could see me, they were signaling.

"Jump, Dylan!" It was Emily. "Quick!"

My feet felt like they were made of concrete. I couldn't move. My lifejacket was gone, and so was my invented courage.

Heavy footsteps thumped toward me and I heard the crabby clatter of Grimdire's armor.

I took a deep breath, filling my lungs with the smoky air as I leaped into the crushing darkness.

✵ 31 ✵

THE LAST FLIGHT

I fell and fell. The air shrieked and gunpowder pricked my nostrils. Booming roars burst from The Rotten Blight and fiery lights flickered across the inky cove. I hit the water hard and sank fast into its cloudy depths.

Everything turned black and still, and for a second I wondered if I'd died.

Panic punched me in the gut. I kicked down and slashed my hands through the water, propelling myself up. I could see a distant glow of fireworks, and hear the hollow booms of cannon fire.

I broke the surface, sucking breath after breath and then slipped back down again. I forced myself back up, flailing as I trod the water.

"Dylan!"

The rowboat rocked and wobbled toward me. Jacob was at the bow, the screen of his phone bright in the gloom. "Dylan!" he called again.

"Here!" I gasped.

The boat vanished and for a moment I was sure they'd

passed me by, but then I heard the splashing oars, and they appeared through the mist.

Zach, Emily and Jacob, they all reached out for me. Their hands were warm as they pulled me up into the boat. I collapsed as cannon fire exploded around us.

"It... it didn't work," I said. "I'm sorry. I blew into it, there was a loud whistle... but nothing happened."

"Be patient, that's what my Nan always tells me," Zach said, "maybe it just takes time." I could tell he was trying to keep our spirits up, but I heard the doubt in his voice. "Look out!" He ducked as a cannon ball whizzed over the boat.

"Move!" Jacob cried.

Zach and Emily seized the oars and rowed into the mist. No one had any idea which direction would take us to shore, or simply away from the Blight, for that matter. But as the fog parted we saw the Strimple's tug boat. Angelina was still taking pot-shots at Grimdire with her rifle, and Fitzroy was now brandishing his shovel.

"They haven't thought that through," Jacob said.

Cannonballs careened toward the Strimples as Grimdire stood at the back of the Blight, raising and dropping his cutlass in time with each roaring blast until one of them finally struck the tug. There was a fiery explosion, and I saw the silhouettes of Angelina and Fitzroy framed against the swirling red and orange blaze as they leaped overboard.

"One down, a few thousand to go!" Grimdire cried. He pointed his cutlass to the quaintly lit town shimmering through the churning mist. The ship began to turn. Its hull swept at us and we nearly capsized as it pointed toward Coupeville like an arrow.

"It's too late!" I said, more to myself than anyone else. I'd failed. People were going to die.

If only I hadn't lost the map...

Coward! It was Jamie's voice, smug and leering as it echoed through my mind. "No," I whispered. I'd been brave. Braver than he could have ever been. But it hadn't helped, not in the end...

"Look!" Emily cried as she pointed to a strange shadow trailing the Blight.

It took a moment to see what she meant. Then the dark water churned and a great tentacle arced up, framed by the glowing mist. A pair of milky-blue eyes shone in the gloomy depths just before it plunged back down beneath the surface.

It looked like the octopus had turned in retreat. My hopes faded fast.

"Yes!" Zach screamed as three tentacles shot up from the water and seized the Blight's mast. Then another pair of snaking arms shot out and grabbed its hull, bringing it to a juddering halt.

Cannons blazed and fired into the cove, but the octopus didn't let go. Bells chimed frantically alongside the panicked cries of the pirates as two more arms burst from the water and seized the stern. Then another soared up smashing the cannons on the port side until they fired no more.

The ship listed toward us while silhouettes of pirates scurried by like rats on the deck. Grimdire fired at every visible part of the beast and his crew did the same, but the octopus took a swipe, knocking them down like bowling pins. Then, with a great wrenching wail, The Rotten Blight began to tip further onto its side.

Jacob seized the oars and spun our boat around to face the galleon as it capsized with an almighty splash. Huge choppy waves roared toward us as it sank. I helped Jacob steady the unwieldy boat as we rolled over the churning white crests. Then we looked back to see The Rotten Blight vanish into the swirling, bubbling water as if it had never existed.

The last I saw of the pirates was their screeching parrot circling like a black shadow in the mist. As we followed its flight, a tentacle shot out of the water and snatched it down into the depths.

"Yes!" Zach shouted. We hollered and cheered until our voices went hoarse. We hugged each other tight and I felt like my face might split from the size of my grin.

"You did it!" Zach said to me.

"What I can't figure out is how the octopus found them," Emily said as we rowed back through the darkness. With the mist gone, I could just about see the lights on the far shore. "I mean the ship had sailed off after you blew into the shell, right?"

"Yeah, but it was still onboard. I dropped it into Grimdire's pocket," I said, allowing myself another smile.

"Nice one! You know, I don't care what anyone else says about you," Zach chuckled as he clapped me on the shoulder, "I think you're pretty cool. And I doubt there'll ever be anyone as smart or heroic as you. They should make a statue of you. No, scratch that, they should make a million. Yeah, that should do it."

It was a crazy statement of course but I decided to remember it the next time Jamie started harping on about what a loser I was.

Finally, we struck shore and Jacob leaped onto the beach before helping us climb out. We dragged the boat back and carefully left everything just as we'd found it.

We'd already made a plan to replace the lifejacket that Grimdire had destroyed, which meant no one would probably ever need to know about what we'd done. The thought of that felt strange, but I decided I could live with it, especially if it meant enjoying a trouble-free summer with my new friends.

We were about to head back to Violet's car when two heavy splashes came from behind us.

An ice-cold shiver ran down my spine. I knew who it was without turning.

The Strimples.

They stormed toward us and I'd never seen anyone looking so crazed and murderous in all my life.

❧ 32 ❧

FIREWORKS

"You've lost us our treasure!" Fitzroy Strimple growled. He clutched a heavy stone, and so did his sister.

"It wasn't your treasure," I called back. I was terrified, but I'd had enough. "And it wasn't Grimdire's loot either. He stole it."

"So what! It was our inheritance and we've been searching for it for years!" Angelina cried. "Ever since we read about it in our grandmama's journals."

"And now it's... it's gone... poof! Like lost dreams!" Fitzroy blurted, showering his fake beard with angry spit.

"Yeah, well you'd better go poof too!" Emily said as she pointed at the boats speeding toward the burning wreckage of their tug. "That's the Coast Guard and the police, I'm pretty sure they're going to want to talk to you."

"We're not going anywhere missy, not without adequate compensation," Fitzroy said.

Zach reached into his pockets. "I've got twenty seven cents. Is that adequate enough for you?" I could hear he was scared, but angry too.

"Not even close," Angelina said, "if all you can scrape up is pennies, then you're going to have to work it off. Like mules. For the rest of your miserable lives."

"Doing what?" Jacob sounded genuinely curious.

"Whatever we see fit!" Fitzroy growled. "Now come with us." He raised his stone.

A strange light caught the edge of Jacob's glasses as he pushed them firmly back on his nose. And then I saw what he was looking at. Three sets of flashlights were sweeping along the cove road, and they were coming our way. Cops.

"Hey!" Jacob cried, "over here!"

Zach, Emily and me joined him.

"Damn your eyes!" Angelina croaked.

"Let's get out of here!" Fitzroy said as they dropped their stones and ran. "We'll be back for you, believe me!" he called over his shoulder.

Jacob reached into his backpack and pulled out what looked like a clunky white plastic gun. He aimed it into the sky and fired.

A bright orange flare shot through the air and soared over the beach, illuminating the retreating Strimples. The cops took off after them and for a moment it seemed like they might get away but then Fitzroy tripped over some driftwood and Angelina flew into him, bringing them both down in a jumble of limbs.

Moments later the cops had them pinned down and were shining flashlights in their faces. One snatched off Fitzroy's fake beard and Angelina's glasses as he called in on his radio. A few moments later they cuffed them.

"Maybe we should go over there?" Jacob said, "we can tell them what happened."

"What, and spill the beans about Captain Grimdire and the giant magical octopus? Are you nuts?" Zach shook his head. "Those turkeys already have a warrant out on them. They're goners and we're golden. Unless we fail to get our butts home before we get grounded."

We turned and ran back to the car. My shoes squelched and my clothes were soaked through. Violet's windows were steamed up and super cheesy music blared from inside her car. It stopped as Zach rapped his knuckles against the window.

"Where have you been?" Violet demanded, "do you know how worried I was?"

"You don't look that worried to me," Zach muttered as looked her in the eye.

"If anything happened to you I'd be in a world of-" She stopped as she noticed Zach waiting for her to say the word.

"Nothing happened. We were just enjoying the fireworks. It's not our fault they were setting them off so late," Emily said as she glanced at each of us. "Right?"

"Yeah," we agreed.

"Yeah," Zach added as he peered into the empty night sky, "it looks like we're all done here. So home now, Vi. Quick smart."

❧ 33 ❧
BACK TO THE SHADOWS

I woke as Emily gently shook my shoulder and handed me a glass of orange juice. It took me a moment to remember where I was and that we'd camped out in the tent below the tree house. Jacob gave me a sleepy nod as he took a long sip of his drink.

"Morning," I said.

I'd borrowed a pair of Zach's pajamas and they were a bit too short in the arms and legs, so I looked like I'd had an overnight growth spurt. My clothes were piled up beside my pillow and they'd been washed and dried. I thanked Emily because I was pretty sure it wasn't Zach or Violet that had done my laundry, and I was really glad I wasn't going to have to go home in the pajamas.

"Hi," Zach said as he walked across the lawn, trailing a long dressing gown behind him. His hair was sticking up all over the place and he sounded kind of bummed out.

"What's up?" Jacob asked. "You should be happy!"

"Zach's never happy," Emily replied.

"I am," he said as he ran a hand through his hair, making it even worse. "But..." he sighed, "no one's ever going to know what we did. I mean, we saved a whole town and defeated Grimdire and got the Strimples arrested but we can't even tell anyone, can we?"

"It's probably best not to," Jacob said as he tied his shoes.

"Not unless we want to end up in the nuthouse," I added.

"Exactly!" Zach said, "Being an unsung hero really sucks. I was hoping for some prestige, maybe a medal or something, you know? And a prize or cash reward would have been nice too."

"But *we* know what we did," Emily said, "and that's what counts."

"Yeah," Zach said, although he didn't sound convinced.

Jacob rolled up his sleeping bag and finished his orange juice. "I should probably head home," he said.

"Yeah, me too," I said as I tidied my sleeping bag and sheets and went to the bathroom to change into my clean clothes.

Jacob and the others were out in the front yard by the time I was done. I picked up my bike. The handlebars were already getting hot in the shining sun.

"Call us later," Zach said. He raised 'Hidden Whidbey's Monstrous Myths and Lofty Legends!' in his hand. "You know, I was flicking through this and I'm thinking it might be a good idea for us to do a little investigation on the Saratoga Sasquatch. What do you think?"

"Sounds good," Jacob said.

Emily rolled her eyes. "I wouldn't go that far."

"I would," I said, "I'd love to find a Sasquatch; I could introduce it to my brother."

We waved as we took off down the driveway, then Jacob and I raced each other down the road, until we were both out of breath. "See you later terminator." he called as I turned to cycle up the hill to my house.

"Yeah, see you later." I laughed.

The sky was huge, blue, and full of possibilities.

⬥

MOM AND DAD WERE AT THE KITCHEN TABLE WHEN I GOT back. Mom glanced up at me over her newspaper. "Did you see it?" Her eyes were wide and her voice excited.

"See what?" I asked.

"The ship!" Dad said, "you went to see the fireworks at Penn Cove last night, didn't you?"

"Yeah," I said. "Why, did I miss something?" I tried to sound casual.

"Only an exploding tug boat," Mom said, nodding to the newspaper.

"And a mysterious, old ship that appeared in the cove in the middle of the night," Dad added.

Right, Grimdire's stolen ship, I'd forgotten about that.

"Here!" Mom thrust the paper at me. "You can read about it for yourself. There's plenty of pictures too."

"Cool, I'll take a look later. Are we out of cereal?" I asked, hoping to change the subject. I'd had enough of pirates to last me a lifetime. I headed upstairs to stash the article away when something wooshed toward me.

I ducked as a frisbee clattered off the wall.

"Got you!" Jamie said. He stood down the hall, his hands glued to his hips in one of his power stances.

"Nope, you missed." And then, almost under my breath I added, "Loser."

He stomped toward me, his face twisted in anger. "What did you call me?" he hissed, making sure Mom and Dad didn't hear him.

I stood my ground. "A loser." I held his gaze. "I've dealt with bigger jerks than you."

"Really?" he demanded. "Like who?"

He pushed me. I didn't budge; I just smiled back at him. "Believe me, you don't want to know. By the way, Jamie, you were right. This island isn't what it seems." I watched as his brow furrowed. For once it seemed he had nothing else to say.

And then I turned, expecting him to shove me, but he didn't. I could hear him shuffling down the hall as I pushed my bedroom door open. It felt good to finally stand up to him. Maybe even better than taking on Captain Grimdire and the Strimples.

⚜

AFTER LUNCH MOM, DAD AND JAMIE WENT OUT FOR another run so I cycled back to Emily and Zach's place and met them in The Towering Lair of Eternal Secrets. Jacob came over too and we spent the day leafing through 'Hidden Whidbey's Monstrous Myths and Lofty Legends' and discussing what to do next. There were so many possibilities that by the time we had to leave, we'd only narrowed our list down to ten different things.

The sky was turning grey as I rode away. I was tired and wanted to go straight home, but I'd brought The Life and Times of the American Toad with me and I wanted to drop it off at the post office so I could be rid of it. Unfortunately it turned out the post office was closed, so given that the map was no longer of any threat or use to anyone as far as I could see, I decided to drop it off at Mr. Ovalhide's house.

Inside the book, along with the map, was the $20 Mr. Ovalhide had given me for the shipping. It seemed only fair to return it. As for the $50, that was gone. We'd spent it on ice-cream and shovels, but I figured we'd more than earned it.

A cool breeze blew as I walked up the drive, causing goosebumps to break on my arms. The house was still dark and filled with shadows, like there was no one living there. I glanced through the window but couldn't see anything so I just slipped the book through the letterbox and listened as it thumped down onto the floor inside.

The place was still beyond creepy and as I walked down the driveway, I felt the dark building looming at my back. Then, as I climbed onto my bike, a single, yellow light flickered on in the upstairs window and a black figure appeared before the glass.

I cycled away.

Fast.

THE END

A PREVIEW OF BOOK TWO OF WEIRDBEY ISLAND - THE DAY OF THE JACKALOPE

THE DAY OF THE JACKALOPE

Chapter One

It was a quiet, cool grey morning and the clouds were so low they seemed to hang over the treetops. It was July but I supposed strange weather was just the way it was living on Whidbey Island, or Weirdbey Island as me, Zach, Emily and Jacob now called it.

I'd been pulling weeds for what seemed like hours and my hands were caked in dirt. The back of my neck itched from mosquito bites, or whatever evil twisted bugs were sneaking up on me and sucking my blood.

Weeding wasn't really how I wanted to spend my summer but mom was paying pretty generously by her standards. With the money I was making, I figured I was about five percent closer to getting the new laptop I wanted, and mom was happy.

Besides that, things had pretty much stalled with our investigations. We'd spent the whole of the week before searching for the Saratoga Sasquatch and the only thing we'd stumbled upon was mud, brambles and horse apples. The lack of results had been frustrating, but I'd enjoyed hanging out with my new friends.

What I wasn't happy about was our super-creepy neighbor, Mrs. Chimes. She'd just driven by our house in her long, shiny chocolate-brown car and slowed as she'd spotted me. Her window had creaked as it slid down and I'd waited for her to say something, anything. But she'd simply watched as I'd pulled out a handful of knotty weeds and a slow grin had spread over her wizened face.

"Morning," I'd called to break the awkward silence.

"Greetings!" she'd replied, and then she'd nodded slowly, like we'd shared something between us before driving off. It had been freaky, but apparently freaky was the norm on Weirdbey Island.

I was about to put on some music to distract myself when two shadows fell over me. One was stocky, the other so long it almost reached the edge of the house. A pang of dread slithered through me as I turned, already knowing who was there.

Jamie's stupid eyes gleamed with mockery. Beside him was his new friend; Marshall Anders. Marshall was a tall boy with a shaved head, dull, almost dead eyes and a face as craggy as the moon.

"The weed's weeding." Jamie sounded pleased with his insult.

"Yep," Marshall agreed. He smiled, but it only lasted a second, like he was trying to hide it. The way they stood made them look like they were up to something.

I ignored them and started working on the flower bed near the drive, where I could keep an eye on them. I didn't want to turn my back on Jamie, not while my parents were out. "I've got stuff to do," I said as they continued watching me.

"Let's leave him to it," Jamie said.

I tried to hide my shudder. Something was definitely up; there was no way he'd leave me alone, not that easily. No, Jamie liked to take his time torturing me, like a cat toying with a mouse.

"Gardening's no fun," Marshall said. "I had to weed my uncle's garden last month. It nearly broke my back." He leaned on the fence and gazed down at me. His face was almost... friendly? "You know, there're easier ways to get money, right?"

"Like what?" I asked. Right away I knew I should have kept my mouth shut. But it was too late, Marshall and I were officially having a chat.

"Like..." Marshall narrowed his eyes, as if deciding whether to tell me something. There was a long pause, and then he said, "like spending five cents and getting a dollar back."

Jamie sighed. "It's probably not working anymore." He pulled his hand from his pocket and his palm was full of shiny dollar coins, like the kind we used to get when we'd lost a tooth. I'd never seen so many in my life.

Marshall checked his phone. "Naw, it should be working again by now. We just needed to give it a rest. Its been at least an hour since the last time we tried it."

"Tried what?" I asked, unable to stop myself.

"The statue," Marshall replied as he pulled a handful of golden dollar coins from his pocket too. "See, I told you, it wasn't a trick." he said to Jamie, "I've still got all mine. They're real." He took one and bit into its side like people did in the movies. "You want some?" he asked me.

"Hey!" Jamie elbowed him in the side. "You said we weren't supposed to tell anyone and now you're bragging about it to that fool."

Marshall shook his head and studied me once more. "He's not so bad, are you?"

I shrugged. I had no idea what they were talking about, but

the money had my interest. Was he really going to share it? I knew the answer already of course, but I could dream.

Marshall glanced around the yard, leaned down even closer to me, and smiled like we were old friends. "Look, if I tell you a secret, do you promise to keep it to yourself? Because-"

"Don't tell him!" Jamie's tone was shrill and whiney.

My curiosity was on fire. "Don't tell me what?"

Marshall glanced around again and lowered his voice. "I'm going to trust you, Dylan."

"Marshall!" Jamie protested.

But Marshall shook his head. "No, I'm telling him. There's enough for all three of us."

"You're as dumb as he is," Jamie muttered. And then Marshall rounded on him and he glanced away. Jamie was tough, but it seemed Marshall was tougher. I suddenly liked him more, despite those weird, dead eyes. Maybe he wasn't so bad after all. "Listen," he continued, "two houses down from here there's a statue of a lady, in the flowerbed on the side of Mr. Flittermouse's house."

"Mr. Flittermouse?" I asked.

"Yeah, just down the road. He's got a rusty old mail box with his name painted on the side, its right there next to his driveway. That's how you'll know you've got the right place. The plants in his yard are really wild and overgrown but you can't miss her."

"Who's the statue of?" I asked.

"His wife," Marshall said, "she died a couple of years back and he had the statue made to remember her by. But here's the interesting thing." He pulled a nickel from his wallet and held it toward me like it was something special. "This will sound crazy, but what you do is put five cents in her hands, close your eyes, and turn around three times. Counter-clockwise, it has to be counter-clockwise, you know what that is, right?"

I nodded. Of course I did.

"Good. So you spin around three times and after you have, the nickel will turn into a golden dollar."

"You're joking, right?" I asked. "You expect me to believe that?"

My confidence melted as Marshall's eyes turned cold and dim once more. "Whatever. It's up to you, man." He shrugged but his face softened a little. "I suppose I didn't believe it when I first heard it either. You know, I was just trying to do you a favor."

"Don't waste your time on him," Jamie said as he began to walk away, "time's money. Literally."

"I guess," Marshall said. And then he paused and flipped the nickel up into the air. It tumbled toward me and I managed to catch it without dropping it. "Give it a try, Dylan," Marshall called as he walked down the trail with Jamie, "what have you got to lose?"

I watched them go, half expecting them to turn and laugh at me, but they continued on their way. Jamie seemed angry, and I heard him mutter "What did you tell him for?"

Marshall answered but his voice was too low to hear as they vanished around the bend in the track.

I turned the coin over several times, inspecting it closely to figure out if they'd done something weird to it, but it didn't have a suspicious mark on it. It was just a plain old nickel. I plunged the trowel into the earth and left it there as I glanced down the lane in the opposite direction. I'd never heard of Mr. Flittermouse, but then again I hadn't actually met any of our neighbors yet, except for Mrs. Chimes.

"What have I got to lose?" I shrugged, adopting Marshall's logic as I tried to persuade myself it was at least worth a try. I sighed, half expecting the worst but secretly hoping for the best as I set off down the trail.

A beam of golden sunlight broke from the clouds and brightened the heavy green branches, as they cast dancing shadows over the ground. Squirrels chased each other across the limbs and a deer stood in the woods watching me. I considered going back to get our dog, Wilson, but he'd probably just be a hindrance, especially if things went wrong.

"Just a quick look," I told myself. "Then I'll get back to the weeding."

The first house I spotted was set back into the trees, but I could see its bright blue paint easily enough. I wondered who lived there and hoped it wasn't Mrs. Chimes, because that would mean she was our next door neighbor. I didn't like that idea one little bit.

Then I came to the next driveway. The pockmarked script on the battered old mailbox read 'Flittermouse'. I glanced along the curved gravel path but it vanished as it wound through the trees. And then my gaze fell on a sign posted on a tall hemlock just a few feet in from the road. It read:

'Trespass at your doom!'

"That doesn't sound very friendly." I glanced at my phone and considered calling Jacob, Zach and Emily, to see if they wanted to come with me. But then I realized, if I extended the invitation to investigate a magic statue that was handing out dollar coins and it turned out to be a hoax, I'd just end up looking like an idiot in front of them as well as Jamie and Marshall.

I rubbed the small of my back. It still ached from the weeding. I wasn't exactly looking forward to finishing the chore, but maybe I wouldn't have to... as unlikely as that was...

"This is so dumb." I started down the driveway, taking care to listen closely. It took a good couple of minutes of walking before I saw the house. It was covered in streaks of green and brown paint. "Who paints their house in...camouflage?" I mumbled.

It was too weird. I was about to turn and head back as fast as I could without running, when I saw a white figure through the trees.

My heart jumped. I stood absolutely still.

Then I realized it wasn't a person, it was the statue.

As I got closer I saw more details. It was a Japanese woman dressed in long robes and her hands were cupped before her. A sword rested at her feet and beside it was a lotus flower floating in an ornate bowl of water.

I listened hard. It seemed I was on my own. I glanced at the house again and realized there were no cars around. Hopefully that meant no one was home.

My attention shifted back to the statue. It couldn't hurt to check it out, could it? I wandered toward it, holding branches back as I stumbled through the tall grass, my eyes fixed on the stone woman. Something silver gleamed in her hand...

A coin!

Maybe Marshall and Jamie hadn't been lying after all.

"Wait," I whispered to myself as I slowed.

Someone else was there. Someone was watching.

I felt their eyes on me but they didn't make a sound, all I could hear was the distant drill of a woodpecker. I decided to go home. Fast.

And then I heard a whisper of movement, but before I could turn two hands clamped down on my shoulders, stopping me in my tracks.

Chapter Two

The hands clenching me smelt waxy and were streaked with woody colors. "Hey!" I yelled as I tried to pull away, but they held me firm. I kicked back and my sneaker struck what felt like a leg.

"Ow!" someone growled.

I spun around and came face to face with an old man dressed head to toe in camouflage. His face was smeared in green, brown and black and he'd even painted the few wisps of hair left on his head.

"Freeze!" he demanded as he waved his hands through the air and let out a slow, controlled breath. "That's right," he said, his voice creaky and gruff, but full of energy, "I move like the wind and dance like the lightning! You didn't see me coming and you never will. I am the tiger. I am the tiger!" He bellowed. He pointed his gnarled forefinger like a dagger. "Now, empty your pockets!"

"Why?" My heart was still racing, but I was more baffled than scared.

"Because I know a slippery customer when I see one, that's why. You have the look of a goat that's gobbled down more than his fair share of grass. Guilty, greedy, a gluttonous gazumper."

"What's a gazumper?"

He continued like he hadn't heard me. "You just wandered down my driveway as jittery as a turkey on Thanksgiving morn, and tried to sneak past me like a cat burglar on springs. But I knew you was on your way before you even thought of it. My mind's as fast as a hurricane and sharper than a particularly sharp knife."

"I don't know that that makes sense," I said, before I could stop myself.

"Perhaps you're feeble minded? The name's Roscoe Flittermouse. You may have heard tell of me."

"Nope."

"Well my enemies have, you can count on that. And you are?"

"I'd expect you to already know who I am, especially if you knew I was on my way here before I even did." I replied. I didn't mean to be snippy, but I was angry. Mostly with myself for letting Jamie and Marshall dupe me into coming here. "Look, I'm sorry Mr. Flittermouse, I was just curious about your statue. I didn't mean any harm."

He studied me for a moment and gave a short sharp nod. "I see this is so, but I still require your name."

"Dylan Wilde."

"Ah, the Wildes. You've just moved into the old Prendergast place," he said, tapping his temple with his index finger as if this detail proved he possessed some sort of eerie mental super powers. "Now, I'm sure you'll understand that I'll need to have words with your parents, but other than that our business is concluded." Then his finger shot through the air like an arrow. "But listen and listen good; do not stray onto my land again. I prowl these woods with the stealth of a flea and the guile of an ancient otter."

"Are you..." I paused as I felt my cheeks reddening. And then I spat out the words as fast as I could. "Are you involved with The Society of the Owl and the Wolf?" He really seemed like he must be.

Mr. Flittermouse laughed theatrically. "Indeed I am not, but I know who they are. Our paths have crossed whilst fighting the darkness that prowls on our beautiful little island. And my oh my is it rising again."

He had my interest. "What do you mean?"

Mr. Flittermouse looked around before lowering his voice. "I mean the disappearances of course. Don't tell me you haven't noticed them."

"Disappearances?"

"People, tourists, locals. Vanishing in the dead of night like a forgotten rumor. Something rotten's a-roosting. Something terrible."

"What?"

Mr. Flittermouse shrugged. "How should I know? I spend my days guarding my trees."

"From what?"

"Theft!"

I glanced around. I couldn't see any tree stumps and I told him so.

"There are no stumps!" he said, as if I was the mad one. "No stumps, no displaced dirt, nothing but absence. One day a tree casts its shadow across the land and sinks its roots into the cool earth. The next it's gone as if it was never there." He leaned low. "I think she's taking them to her secret grove."

"Who?"

He laughed and tapped the side of his nose. "I'll not speak her name in the open. Let's just say she rings like a bell."

I thought about it. Chimes. "Mrs.-"

"Nope! Don't say it."

"She's taking trees and people?" Things were getting stranger and stranger.

"I never said she's the one stealing people. But I know for a fact she's got her grim sights set on my trees. No, the kidnapper, or peoplenapper to be more accurate, is a different force of darkness entirely."

"Right." I nodded. I hadn't heard of anyone going missing, and I couldn't see any evidence that his trees had been taken either. He was as mad as a box of frogs, it was as simple as that. "Look, I'm sorry I wandered up your driveway. It won't happen again."

"It better not. Now off with you, vamoose, scram!" Mr. Flittermouse lunged forward and pointed toward the road.

I stumbled through the undergrowth. When I looked back, he'd already gone. I wasn't surprised.

By the time I got home, Mr. Flittermouse had somehow gotten to my house and told my mom everything that had happened. She stood in the yard, arms folded, her face reddening, which was never a good sign. Jamie's head poked from the window behind her. He beamed a big cheesy grin at me. I ignored him.

"Well?" Mom asked.

"Erm, did, er, Mr. Flittermouse-"

"Yes. He kindly stopped by and explained you'd been interloping on his sacred earth. Those were his exact words."

"Look, I'm sorry. I just..."

"Just what?"

"I was just looking for something?" I tried to ignore Jamie as he mimed laughing behind mom. She spun around, as if sensing his stupidity, but by the time she'd turned he'd vanished.

"So what exactly were you looking for? And why?"

"I heard there was something in Mr. Flittermouse's garden... I don't know."

"And who exactly told you there was *something... I don't know* in Mr. Flittermouse's garden?"

"Just someone." Despite my anger I had no intention of snitching. For one thing, Jamie would make my life miserable once he caught up with me. For another, I didn't want his creepy friend Marshall on my case either.

"You're too easily influenced, Dylan. You need to learn to think for yourself." Mom's tone was softer now.

I nodded. "Sorry."

"Well, you've been warned. And if I hear you've been wandering onto other people's properties again, I'll ground you. Is that clear?"

I nodded again, like one of those toy dogs people put in the back window of their cars.

"You've got to be more careful, Dylan. There are strange people in this world. Do you understand me?"

Truer words were never spoken. "I do. Sorry, Mom."

She glanced at the garden where I'd dug out the weeds. "You did a good job. Now go inside and wash your hands, okay?"

I did as she said and refused to meet Jamie's eye as he watched from the doorway of his room. "Sucks to be you, Dylaboo!" he whispered.

Yeah, but only when you're around, I thought to myself.

I cleaned up, flopped down on my bed and read. After a while Wilson wandered in and tried to wash my feet. "What's up, boy." I scratched his ear and was thinking about taking him for a walk when the phone rang. A moment later Jamie shoved my door open and hurled the phone at me. "It's one of your idiot friends,' he said, loud enough for whoever was calling to hear.

"Your brother's a jerk," Zach said, as I answered the phone. "I should probably challenge him to a duel or something."

"You'd lose," I said.

"Maybe, maybe not. Anyway, that's not why I'm calling." I could hear cars and the distant squawk of gulls as he paused.

"So what do you want?" It seemed like it always took Zach forever to get to the point whenever he phoned.

"Uh, I just heard some very interesting news... We're heading over to the beach in Langley. You've got to get over there right now and meet us!"

"What is it?" I sat up fast. Wilson scrambled across the floor.

"Someone said they saw a mermaid, Dylan. A mermaid!"

Chapter Three

The breeze riffled my hair as I cycled through town, zipping past the parked cars. Langley was quiet, probably because it was a weekday and the grey sky carried the threat of rain.

My wheels juddered as I shot down the slope leading to the beach and passed by a bunch of people standing in a rough circle on the grassy path. I wondered if they were whale watchers, then I thought they might be looking for Zach's mermaid. Not that I was totally convinced it was real. But they weren't looking at the beach, they were looking at each other. Weird.

"Hey!" I hit my brakes as two rabbits darted in front of me, one fluffy and orange, the other speckled grey. They didn't even hesitate and with a sharp thrust of their hind legs they leaped over the long grass and vanished into the brush. I'd seen loads of them around town and I'd kept meaning to ask the others where they'd all come from.

The question slipped from my thoughts once again as I spotted Zach and Emily standing at the shoreline. Zach was pointing into the sea as the wind whipped along and sent his hair snaking up over his head. He lifted the bulky old fashioned camera he'd taken to wearing around his neck and started snapping away. I had no idea why he didn't just use his phone but he never seemed to do anything the normal way.

Something dark moved in the water before them. A head? Was someone swimming? No. I could see a tail...

I dropped my bike. "What is it?" I called.

Zach turned and grinned. "That's the hundred million dollar question."

The tide was coming in fast and the wind made the water choppy and white capped, causing the thing floating out there to sink below the waves. Whatever it was, it seemed lifeless. Dead. I shivered.

Shhhhhhh

I turned as Jacob shot toward us on his mountain bike, which always made mine look like a filthy relic. "What is it?" he asked as he leaned his bike on its stand and adjusted his glasses.

"A mermaid," Zach said, "I think…"

"It's not a mermaid," Emily said to Zach, her tone irritable, like she'd been telling him the same thing over and over. Her arms were folded tight, and she rolled her eyes as she glanced at me and Jacob.

"It's not a mermaid," Zach repeated, mimicking her voice until she elbowed him in the ribs.

"Whoa!" I said as a wave lifted it up and I caught a glimpse of long blonde hair and a shadowy face. Then a great silvery tail splashed behind the creature. For some reason the thing, whatever it was, was wearing a blue T-shirt.

It vanished under the rolling waves then bobbed along and washed up on the beach before us.

"Ugh!" Emily held a hand over her nose and mouth.

"Oh man, that thing stinks! I gasped.

"It's dead…" Zach said, "poor thing!"

"It can't be dead," Jacob said and sighed. "It was never alive. Not in its current form, anyway." He gingerly placed his foot on the side of the body and rolled it over, causing Zach to scream even louder than Emily.

I stared with horror into its monkey-like face, as scales slipped from its body and glittered on the sand. The logo on the T-shirt read, 'Bobby Spigot's Fish n' Chip Haven!"

"What the-" Zach's words tailed off as he stared down, stupefied.

"Ever hear of the Fiji Mermaid?" Jacob asked.

"Nope," I said.

Jacob held his phone studiously between his finger and thumb and began snapping photos. "They were sideshow exhibits back in the olden days. Touted as mermaids, but really it was just a hoax. People that are into taxidermy would call it a gaff. It's the top half of a monkey sewn onto the body of a big fish. But whoever made this one did a sloppy job. Look you can see the stitches by that fin."

"Why would anyone want to make something like that?" Emily's voice was riddled with disgust.

"Just as a curiosity I suppose, but I think this one's supposed to be some kind of marketing stunt," Jacob said as he examined the pictures he'd just taken. "It'll go viral alright, but for all the wrong reasons." He laughed.

"What should we do with it?" Zach asked. He sounded almost as disappointed as he was revolted.

"Chuck it in the trash so it's not littering the beach," Emily suggested.

"Or giving people nightmares," Jacob added.

"Too late. I'm going to have nightmares for the rest of my life," Zach said. He prodded it with his foot and it rolled over. "Hey, it's really light!" He nodded Emily. "Grab it by the tail Em and we'll get rid of it."

"Ha! Why don't you grab it?" Emily asked, glaring back at him.

Zach looked over to Jacob and I, sighing like a world-weary old man as we shook our heads no. "Produce the coin of fate if you would, coin master," he said to Jacob.

Jacob dipped into his pocket and pulled out the quarter he kept for occasions such as this, and there were plenty. "Heads," he called as we made our bets.

After two more rounds Jacob proved the loser. He lifted the mermaid from the sand with care.

"Look, now you've both heads and tails at the same time, Jacob," Zach laughed.

Jacob rolled his eyes. "Wow, you're right." He said. "It's super light. The inside must be made of cork or something," Then he carried it across the beach, accepting his fate gracefully even as Zach took pictures and congratulated him on his bride-to-be.

Zach wheeled Jacob's bike along and Emily gave us all a wide berth as she cast sidelong glances at the creature. "I need something to take my mind off that thing," she said as we walked back toward town.

"Like what?" I asked.

"I dunno. Maybe we could get a milkshake. You owe me one, Zach, remember?"

He looked glum as he shrugged. "I guess. But are you sure you want to cash that favor in? It'll probably be lumpy or soured. Nothing's going right today. We can't even get a decent lead on anything."

"Well, as far as I'm concerned the case of the Weirdbey mermaid was just solved. So I for one feel motivated," Emily said to Zach and then they started sniping at each other as we headed toward the hill.

"Excuse me?"

I glanced up as a middle-aged couple approached us. They seemed startled and worried. Had they seen the mermaid? No, they weren't even looking at it.

"Hi," I said.

"Hi," the woman answered as she tucked her hair behind her ear and regarded us carefully. "We're looking for our mother." She held a phone up. The picture on the screen was of her and the man beside as well as an older lady with thin white hair. "Have you seen her?" she asked.

"No, sorry," I said.

The others peered at the image and shook their heads.

"Oh. Well thank you for your time," the woman said.

"It's her birthday" the man explained as he scanned the beach, "we brought her here to celebrate."

"To the beach?" Zach asked.

"No," the woman smiled, but it didn't last long. "To the island. We're staying at the motel, and when we went to meet up with her this morning she was gone."

"All her things are still there, her suitcase and purse," the man added, "but she didn't leave a note or anything. It's not like her to just disappear."

I thought back to what Mr. Flittermouse had said, about how people were going missing. I almost said something, but bit my tongue. It didn't seem like a good time to mention it.

"We'll keep an eye out for her," Zach said. "We're experienced at solving all kinds of mysteries, actually." He pulled a shiny black slip of paper from his pocket.

"What's that, Zachary?" Emily asked, her voice low.

"My business card. I got a good deal from the printers." Zach nodded to the man as he took the card.

"Zachary Brillion, Legendary Investigator, Pirate Slayer, Twenty-Four Hour Innovator. No job too large, small or medium." I... erm, well that's good to know. Thank you," the man gave a distracted nod as he pocketed the card.

"Yes, thank you for your time," the woman added. And then she glanced at the mermaid cradled in Jacob's arms and without another word they hurried away.

Jacob turned toward us. "I really need to get rid of this thing," he said holding the mermaid as far from his nose as possible.

They all headed towards town. I was about to join them when I spotted something gleaming in the sand. I'd been collecting sea glass as well as oddly shaped pebbles and skimming stones for years, and it looked like I'd just struck gold.

I headed over to the patch of sand and pulled the glass out carefully. It was soft and glinted emerald green in my hand. Then I noticed a few more pieces nearby. I scooped them up, rubbed the damp gritty sand off and held them up to the bright spot of sun glowing through the clouds.

When I looked back the others were halfway up the slope. I placed the sea glass in my pocket, hopped onto my bike and cycled to catch up.

I was at the foot of the slope when I spotted the circle of people from earlier. They were still standing halfway up the grassy path. Now they were humming as they faced each other, and their strange grins were almost as creepy as the way they were gazing into each other's eyes.

And then a tall woman with big black glasses turned from the group and pointed right at me. "Come to us!" she called. "Now!"

———————————————————

The Day of the Jackalope is available from all good bookshops

THE PIRATES OF PENN COVE IS NOW AVAILABLE ON AUDIBLE!

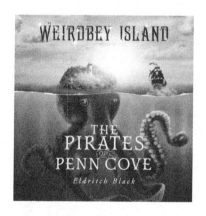

You've read the book, now experience the adventure in audio. Each of the characters have been brought to life in a entirely new way by the fabulously talented narrator J. Scott Bennett. Visit https://eldritchblack.com/audio-books to hear a sample now!

AFTERWORD

Thank you so much for reading The Pirates of Penn Cove, I hope you enjoyed the adventure! If you have a moment, I'd deeply appreciate a quick online review, even a sentence or two would be hugely helpful to pass on the word!

All the best,

Eldritch

BOOKS BY ELDRITCH BLACK

ABOUT THE AUTHOR

Eldritch Black is an author of dark, whimsical spooky tales. His first novel 'The Book of Kindly Deaths' was published in 2014, and since then he's written a number of novels including 'The Day of The Jackalope', 'The Island Scaregrounds', 'Krampus and The Thief of Christmas' & 'The Clockwork Magician'.

Eldritch was born in London, England and now lives in the United States in the woods on a small island that may or may not be called Weirdbey Island. When he isn't writing, Eldritch enjoys collecting ghosts, forgotten secrets and lost dreams.

Connect with Eldritch here:
www.eldritchblack.com
eldritch@eldritchblack.com

Made in the USA
Monee, IL
31 October 2023

45454354R00132